Bringing Out the
Goddess in You

L . C H I L D S

PAGE PUBLISHING, INC.
Conneaut Lake, PA

First originally published by Page Publishing 2020

ISBN 978-1-6624-1440-4 (pbk)
ISBN 978-1-6624-1441-1 (digital)

Printed in the United States of America

Taking a new step, uttering a new word, is what people fear most.
—Benjamin Desrali

This book is dedicated to all who are going to enjoy the read!

"Don't allow regrets from the past or worries about the future define your life in the present. Live with grace and peace, embracing each new day as a gift from God."—Dave Willis

Attention Getter

"Yes, that's what…Damn, baby, you have me…so… OMG, what are you doing to me? It feels so good! Keep going, yes, just like that."

He says, "Shhh, baby, we can't make too much noise or people will hear us. We don't want anyone to know what we're doing in here."

She replies, "Take me to where I need to be, baby. You know how I like it and you know how I want it. I want to see your eyes when you take me there. I want you to relish in the feeling that's going to come with it."

He comes up from giving her the most orgasmic oral experience. As he tosses her to the wall, he gags her mouth with his fingers, giving her something to suck on to keep her quiet as he is about to give her the passion of his pleasure. He's so hard and can't wait to enter her flowing stream of delight. Anticipating the feeling of the warmth that is going to wrap around him, he decides to finger her, making her want him even more. Her body is on the verge of trembling and almost ready to climax. He tells her, "Don't you dare come yet, not until I tell you to." She bites down on his fingers to let him know that she is in a state of an ecstasy emergency and wants to feel every inch of him. Her body temperature was at its all-time high; the feeling on the inside of her was on fire and ready to explode. The thought of him being inside her and touching her walls as she's wrapped all around him turned her on so much she felt like overthrowing him and taking complete control of the sexual situation, just so she can fulfill the need of her body, which was craving him so strongly. The goddess in her was making her want him more than wanting to release in pleasure. Her body temperature was so high she didn't know how much more teasing she would be able to handle before she screamed. He knew how to push her to her limits. He knew how to make her want him like no other. He loved being in control, pushing her to the edge. He could see it in her eyes and body language; she was ready, more than ready for his entrance. The moans, the movement, and the temperature from her body excited him. Being able to make her body tremble and sweat with the energy of wanting him makes him feel like a king.

As she had a mouthful looking deep into his eyes, feeling the masses of his fingers going in and out of her, she turned away, pulling his fingers out of her mouth and said, "Yes, daddy, I want you to give it to me like I've been a bad girl who needs to be punished. I want you to bend me over and spank me as you pull my hair and ask me, 'Who's your daddy?' I love to feel you inside me. You fill me up and you stroke me so good. I love it when you give it to me like that."

As he stared back into her eyes, listening to her, he covered up her mouth with his hand as he placed himself inside of her very slowly, feeling her body tremble from anticipation she relinquishes herself to him with all the anticipation that was built up inside of her. He thrust her deeply and pulls himself out, teasing her, making her body tremble from excitement. He puts her down and turns her around, placing a gag ball in her mouth, latching it in place as he grinds up against her, keeping her body anticipating his reentry. He bends her over, telling her, "Grab your ankles, and don't move them until I tell you to." He enters her, thrusting her slow, hard, and deep. She's practically ready to run from the feeling and thrust he is giving her. It feels so good, and he feels bigger than usual, almost too much for her to take. As he pulls back to thrust her again, he can feel her stream flowing all over him and down her legs. He goes deeper and harder, giving her all of him, admiring in the passion he has released from her.

She moans from the feeling and the sensation that is going through her body, making her weak and ready to climax. This feeling she is feeling she has never felt before, and she's not sure what to do with the emotions and feelings flowing through her. She moans loudly from the pleasure. She wants to move her hands and play with her clit so she can climax faster, but as her daddy has instructed her, she cannot move her hands.

He thrives in all her passion, loving how he can make her flow like the Niagara Falls. He tells her, "Put your hands on the wall and hold steady." She does as she is told, and he slowly increases his speed. He reaches around and grabs her breast, fondling while kissing and sucking on the back of her neck. She feels so good to him; the cushion of her walls makes him weak, and his body is beginning to tremble from the excitement of his orgasm. He holds back, trying hard not to come. He begins to play with her clit; as he plays with it, he feels her body getting weak and trembling, ready to release the energy that's built up inside of her from him making her feel like she is about meet the god of ecstasy.

He asked, "Are you ready, baby? Are you going to show me how I make you feel?" She replies by shaking her head up and down. He told her, "Let's come together, baby." He grabs her hair, thrust her deep and hard, giving her all of him. They come together; bodies are intertwined and getting weak, and the release of all the intensity that's been built up from anticipation has finally fallen for the both of them.

As they both catch their breath and gather their things, they talk about how exciting it was and how they want to do it again. The next time, they are going to go to a little secluded place in the building. As they walk out of the janitor's closet, they go their separate ways to get back to work. The excitement of all that has happened is going to go through both of their minds as they finish out the workday.

That was the best lunch break they've had in a long time. This is going to make a good dinner conversation piece when they get home tonight.

I hope I have your attention now. I more than also hope you enjoyed what you've just read. I wanted to write a book which will capture your attention and keep you interested in reading. Now it's time to get down to the nitty-gritty of things and what this book is about. Please enjoy all that you read, and I hope I was able to open your mind and intrigue you with what I've written. My intent is to help you to help yourself and your relationship or the next relationship you get into.

Please enjoy all that lies ahead in this little book that was written. Take your time to read, and always keep an open mind!

Preface

Who likes to talk about sex? Hey now, I know I do. Sex is, by far, one of my favorite subjects to talk about—next to food! There is nothing wrong with talking about sex, especially with the one you're with. I'm a little unorthodox at times but I'm 100 percent real with it. There's nothing wrong talking about sex among friends and/or family as long as you don't share your intimacies about your relationship with others. I find with some people that they don't like to talk about it because it makes them uncomfortable, and sex should only be talked about with your spouse/significant other. Talking about sex should never be uncomfortable. Sex is an expression of yourself and what you like, how you like it, and what you want to experience sexually. Now I would go as far as to say that talking about the sex you and your mate have with each other—i.e., how great the sex is, his/her private parts, etc.—is not up for discussion, but sex, in general, should be an open topic to talk about. Granted we all have talked about sex from the past with an old fling to other people going into small details about the sex, but NEVER should you discuss the sex in which you are currently having with your spouse/significant other to anyone. There are a lot of people out there you may call your friends and they may envy you in some form or fashion or they could be jealous of you. Never underestimate the friend.

I find *(in my opinion)* sex is a subject that's exciting, refreshing, and inspiring to talk about. Reason being that you can get ideas, inspiration, and input from others on things you have wanted to try but was unequivocally sure of. To be honest, I'm not a big talker at all, especially around people I don't know. I've had to learn a lot of things over the past years about socializing. I like people, but I don't like people. Yes, I said that in the same breath. I know it may sound crazy, but that's how it is.

Before I started to write this book, I was a cosmetologist (still licensed), and I love to do hair; unfortunately, hair is attached to people, so I do what I love to do. I learned how to listen and help others as they would sit in my chair and come to me with their problems. Being a cosmetologist, you get to hear a lot about people's personal lives, their problems, their adventures, what was good, what was not so good, medications they're taking, etc. So with all that being said, not only did I become a good listener but I also became a counselor.

Growing up, I learned how to think outside the box (at a young age), I've learned how to be a better listener, I've learned about myself as a person as I grew older; the more I learned, the better I became. I've also learned about my own likes and dislikes. Life has taught me so many new things about myself it's unfathomable. I also noticed my taste in men and food have changed drastically since I have gotten older, but not for liver. I still don't like liver! There are things I found out about myself I didn't even know. I had to take a self-discovery lesson in life at a couple turns and what I've found out is that I am one AWESOME person! I say it with all the confidence in the world. I am perfectly flawed, and I am better than I was before.

Life is the best teacher you could have no matter if you like what you are going through, what you've accomplished, or what's going on in your life right now; you learn from all of it. Some things you go through in life put you in those situations you don't need to be in, but it's a lesson you need to learn from. Some things you go through you just have to deal with in some kind of way, and maybe you had no hand in how it was dealt to you. Life teaches you all about problem-solving and finding solutions for certain things in life, whether the lesson is for you or for you to teach or talk to someone else about in the long run. With life there are so many times where you are not sure why you go through certain situations or certain pathway's but it's something you have to do.

When it comes to talking about sex, you can learn about different positions, places to have sex, what inspires people to have sex, how much people have sex, how much they would like to have sex, how much they do have sex, who they would like to have sex with, what turns them on/off, what part of sex they like the most, what they would like to try, what they have tried, threesomes, an orgy, orgasms, desires, fantasies, and almost anything that you would like to know and or experience for yourself.

I wrote this book for couples. Married couples and people who are in a relationship and have been in one for a long time—long enough to have already been married but aren't. This is for you!

I wish I could fix every relationship problem, but unfortunately, I can't. I want to help those I can, and if this book helps you out in any way, shape or form at all, I am grateful for what I was able to do. It puts a smile on my face just to know that someone will get something out of this book. I am happy to help whoever I can help in their time of need. I am the kind of person who likes to see other people happy, especially when they are in a marriage or a long-term relationship. I think the things in life that make people happy are food, good conversations, and sex—really good sex and food.

So let's see what this book has to offer!

MARRIAGE IS NOT 50/50
DIVORCE IS 50/50
MARRIAGE IS 100/100
IT ISN'T DIVIDING EVERYTHING IN HALF, BUT
GIVING IT EVERYTHING YOU'VE GOT.

—DAVE WILLIS

Insight

ABOUT ME

It's only right for me to give you some background about myself before you get started reading on what I have to say. I am a tomboy/lady. I know, you're like, how is that even possible? Well, it's hard to explain in some terms, so you will find out as you read—at least I hope you will. I'm not married, but I'm in a relationship. I have five beautiful grown children (four daughters and one son, who is the youngest) and three granddaughters whom I love to death.

I speak, I like to speak raw and uncut. I don't like to sugarcoat or beat around the bush about anything. I find that beating around the bush makes things a lot harder and more confusing than they need to be, and it also makes me exhausted. Also, beating around the bush can make others come up with different conclusion about the factor at hand, so you have to keep things clear and concise. Most people will tell you "just tell me the truth," and when you tell them the truth, they seem to get upset and angry about what they ask for or when it hurts their feelings. I will say, it's better to have your feelings hurt by the truth than to be told a bold-faced lie. Better yet, if you don't want the truth, don't ask me; being brutally honest is a gift of mine. You can learn a lot and change from the truth, or you can be razed and hurt more so from a lie rather than the truth. It is better to hurt from the honest truth (in my opinion). At least give me the option of either dealing with the situation and knowing what's going on because if you lie to me, you break all trust and respect, and that is hard to build back.

What people fail to realize is this: a person can't handle anything and everything raw because they weren't raised or taught to take anything bluntly. So sometimes, you have to find creative ways to say things to someone, especially if they're really sensitive about their feelings. Either constructive criticism or truth about whatever it is you wanted to know about, what you do with that information is totally up to you! However the case may be, you have to face the facts. The one thing I learned how to do when someone would ask me a question would be to phrase my response like this: "Don't take this in a negative way but…" or I would give them the answer and say, "I could not think of a nicer way to say it." But however the answer, I am always truthful, and they know it. I spared their feelings as much as possible. Not everyone processes information the same way; some of us have more filters than others, and we don't hear things the same.

I have always wanted to write a book; even as a child, I knew I wanted to write. I remember getting writing assignments in school, and they would tell us we had to write one-page essay. Mine would be at least three, and my teacher would make me go back and redo it. She would tell me, "You only need the important parts." I would think to myself, *All of what I wrote is important.* So I would go back and redo the entire paper all over again, noticing some of what I wrote was a little repetitive. It would take me the entire weekend to get the paper down to one page; it nearly killed me, but truth of the matter was, I learned how to take out all the unnecessary information and keep the needed information.

I never kept a diary as a child or teenager; I didn't keep a journal about anything. I thought it would be a good idea for me to do (as a kid), but I was too busy being a tomboy: climbing trees and playing marbles, hot wheels, remote-controlled train, remote-controlled race-track, etc. But being a kid, I had nothing to write about and no story to tell. I could have kept a journal about what I did all day every day, but even to me that was boring. As a kid growing up, I liked to write, but who wants to read about playing all day? Nobody! Had I kept a journal or diary at a young age, I possibly would have been able to read some of the memories in which I have totally forgotten. I didn't have the best childhood and I'm sure I didn't have the worst. Then as a teenager, I was just starting to live life and still had nothing to write about, considering I hadn't fully experienced life; life in itself was just getting started!

As I have gotten older and look back on things, I see that life has taught me a lot of valuable lessons and given me insights and food for thought, especially on what it is I want to accomplish and achieve. This book was the first step. You have to go through certain things in life to open your eyes; you have to go through life in order to experience and to see what it has to offer you. Most of us have wool pulled over our eyes or we refuse to see things that are right in front of our face. Sometimes what is obvious seems to be too easy; what's easy is not always obvious. Usually what's right in front of our face, we seem to be in denial or oblivious to, or we brush it off like it's not there and turn a blind eye to it. We brush it under the rug so to speak.

Why did I decide to write about marriage or relationships and sex even though I'm not married, you ask? That's a good question. Personally, I would like to say that I'm a person who likes to think from different angles and get input from everyone. To be frank and honest, I love sex! I like to have sex and I like to talk about sex. That could be an understatement. I talk about sex passionately. I have talked to men and women alike to see what it is that attracts them, turns them on and off, what they are looking for, why they do the things they do when it comes to relationships, good or bad. Not to mention my own experiences, which I have incorporated in this book. I will talk to anyone about sex if they are willing to talk about it. I may not talk about certain things to certain individuals, but sex is always a good topic for me.

Let's start from the beginning, shall we?

THE BEGINNING: HOW IT STARTED

I fell madly in love at the young and tender age of fifteen; I was nuts about a guy whose name I will not mention, but for the fun of it, let's call him Ding Dong! Who hasn't fallen in love at a young age? I was head over heels for him, loved him with all my heart and soul. He was my world, and in my eyes, he could do no wrong. In just that instance, I had wool pulled over my eyes, considering he could do no wrong. I was only fooling myself but didn't know it yet! I didn't let others tell me anything negative about him; although he was cheating on me, I refused to believe it. If there was no proof, then I saw it as a rumor and others trying to cause confusion in our relationship. The only way for me to believe it was to see it with my own eyes. He was my all, my everything, and nothing could break the bond I had with him—the bond we had together (we dated for two years). We did everything together; he would pick me up from school and take me shopping, and we would go to the movies, go out to eat, go bowling, and be together on the weekend. As I saw it, he spent too much time with me in order for him to cheat. You want to talk about someone being foolish and stupid, well, then again, love can make you do things you never thought you would do for anyone when you're young and you're stupid. Let me rephrase that, when you're young and you're ignorant because you don't know any better.

One day, Ding Dong called me on the phone (he was away at a culinary arts school out of state) and told me he was in love with someone else. That sent me to a place I had never been before. Needless to say, I was furious, livid, angry, hurt, and distraught; and I felt like I was about to die. I cried for two weeks behind this man (what I thought was a man). He hurt me to the core of my being. After two weeks of crying and months of being hurt, sad, feeling sorry for myself, and lovesick, I got up and could not believe I was still alive. I didn't think I would be able to live my life without him, but there I was, still alive and breathing. I cried on and off throughout the months ahead, but eventually, the crying came to a complete halt.

My heart was no longer in existence. Let me try to explain to you how it felt or, in other words, how it changed my life. I made it to a point in my life where I was numb. I did not and could not feel; it felt like the Hiroshima bomb was dropped on my heart and leveled it out to ground zero. There was so much radiation that went on for over a period of time *(twenty-plus years)*. My heart was no longer there; it was a desert. I could not feel; I had no emotions. I had NOTHING!

I decided to develop a plan; that plan was to make a man like me fall in love with me and then make him hurt like hell and to see that I was unobtainable. I made every other man pay for the mistake, hurt, and pain Ding Dong caused me.

Unintentionally, I was directing my anger at everyone else and not at the one that hurt me.

Yes, I know this was not fair to others, but I was livid, and I thought, after that, every man was the same. Like I said before, life is a great teacher. I did learn later in life that it was not the right thing to do, although I justified my actions to myself every step of the way. As a teenager, I had a plan, and I was out for revenge. My retaliation on others did not repair the damage that was done to me because it was not directed at the person who hurt me. But I can tell you that I have no regrets about what I did. As I got older, I can see what I did was wrong, and I wasted a lot of my life living in the past and allowing Ding Dong have that much power over me, power he had no idea he had.

This is when I planned my revenge. I was young and had an inquisitive mind, and not to mention, I was very vindictive and conniving. I had a lot of guy friends, so I would listen to them talk about the women they'd been with. They would talk on and on how they would get girls to do things for them, how they would lie to get sex, and how they would *break things off* with them and move on to the next one.

I thought, if men can do these things to women, then why can't women do the same to men? Double standards come into play. Women who get around and sleep with different men are labeled. Women get a bad name when we do the same thing men do. It's okay for a man to be a womanizer, but it is not okay for a woman to treat men like a piece of meat when they act like a piece of meat. With that being said, I did not care what others thought of me and what I was doing. I had a plan I had to follow, and I needed to do something about what was done to me.

I would like to take a step back for a minute. I am not an only child; I do have brothers and sisters. Although we were not raised in the same household, we do keep in touch. I was raised (if you want to call it raised) by my egg donor's mother (grandmother). Most of the time, I was home alone and had to do things on my own. We all come from somewhere, and we all have some kind of background, which is how we grow to be who we are. I had to learn a lot on my own and teach myself how to deal with my emotions and feelings. Growing up, I was told that a closed mouth doesn't get fed. In other words, you need to speak up and speak for yourself. With that being said, as I have grown up and gotten older, I have not bitten my tongue about anything, so I speak my mind, and I speak about how I feel. It's not good to hold in or hold onto animosity, hurt, stress, or grief or whatever it may be. With all that being said, let's get back to it.

Forget the fact that rumors of me being a hoe, slut, tramp, whore, and bitch were going to commence. I HAD TO do some damage because I, of course, was a woman scorned, pissed off, hurt, damaged, and distraught. Guys didn't know that there were women out here that can do the same things they can do. Women are just more elegant and low-key with their dirty laundry. None of the guys I messed with learned that there are other girls that you can't bring home to Mama. They didn't warn you about people like me, and if you did get a warning, you never saw me coming. I was the lad your mother wanted you to bring home. I am the one she wanted to see you settle down with and raise a family. I am the one she wanted to have over during the holidays, spending time with the family. I portrayed to be that perfect girl, you know the "good girl." I was polite, kind to the eyes, respectful, funny, and fun to be around. I was the face of perfection and the ideal candidate.

I devised a plan and tried it out on a few men. When you come up with an idea, you have to do a test run first to work out all the kinks and flaws and, not to mention, to see if it works at all. I had to do a test run on a few people to see how this all was going to work. I tweaked and retweaked it until I mastered my plan and put it into action completely. It became so natural to me; the most dangerous part of all it became who I was. I was perfection; I was how I saw deceitful perfection. I perfected how to be a beautiful, deceitful temptress; and I did it very well, if I should say so myself. I tried to convince myself that I should lie as I went along as my plan was in action. I thought about how all the guys talk to one another and how they lie and tell women what they want to hear. I had to do something different; I wanted to go about this and not lie. I wanted to gain all their trust and make them feel confident. I wanted them to believe in me and what was to come (from their own perspective, as I had a different agenda). There were a few lies here and there as I had to tell them what they wanted or needed to hear, and what I had to lie about most was me "loving" them. What I did not have to lie about was me wanting sex or intimacy. I paid attention to their actions and the words they spoke, and at times, you have to take into consideration what they don't say. It was all a big game for me, and I played that game so well.

I became a ***professional deceitful heartbreaker***. There is nothing more undeserving than to have your heart broken by someone you care about!

Growing up as a child, I used to hear the older people say, "She is going to be a heartbreaker when she grows up." As a kid, I never knew what that meant until I got older and I was hurt by a man. Now I am not sure if that was the way it was supposed to go, but that surely is the direction it went.

I had played that game for twenty-plus years of my life, and for a long time, it did not bother me at all. I don't know if I should call it a game because it became who I was, a part of my life I embraced it wholeheartedly. I was numb all over and the thought of me hurting a man's feelings meant absolutely nothing to me. After all, I was out for revenge, right?

That's a big part of my life that's missing, maybe not so much missing but a lot of time not being able to and not wanting to love again. All the time I spent being so deceitful took a lot of my life away from me when I could have been enjoying life. I could have learned how to forgive and forget, but I was so very stubborn, arrogant, and always looked for a way to get revenge. Revenge on all the men that had, at some point, done someone wrong. I would inquire about stories of men and their past relations to get some insight. (You know, people don't tell all the story; they only tell part of it. Most leave out a lot of what they did and how they reacted to the situation.) So there were many of times I filled in the blanks and played them off what they told me. The thought of someone getting the best of me really bothered me, so I could not let that happen. Although the revenge I took was not taken out on the man that hurt me initially, it felt good to do some damage to someone. Well, in this case, a lot of someones.

I cheated on the boyfriends I had, and if they tolerated it, then so be it. (Now I let them think we were together, but in actuality, I was single and the thought of "us" as a couple appeased their minds). It was nothing for me to push on to the next man considering I had no ties. I didn't care about who I hurt in the process. Then I came to realize, in the long run, that not only did I hurt others but I was also hurting myself. I hurt myself more in the long run and did more damage than I had ever imagined. I did not anticipate on doing any damage to myself. I was not looking that far ahead. I also did not think I would have carried on as long as I did. My deceitfulness got the very best of me; all that time is gone away, and there is no way for me to get it back.

I never thought that I would end up doing so much damage to myself in the long run. I didn't think I would have to recover from myself. I began to think later in life I wanted to be able to settle down and have a man to call my own. I wanted to be able to be with someone whole- heartedly—no games, no lies, no deceit, just real love and compassion for each other. I was so used to being another person, doing what I had done for all those years. I had no clue as to what I was up for when it came to being in a real relationship. I tentatively became another person all together, and I was not sure how to undo what I had done to myself. Talk about self work! I didn't know how hard it was going to be to undo my alternate ego and repair myself to be able to open up again. I had to get out of and let go of all the bad habits and the change of lifestyle..

At that time, I was comfortable in my lifestyle and saw nothing wrong with the way I was living. Not only was I comfortable with my lifestyle, but it also became who I was. Trying to change from who you've become to become someone else is a very difficult assignment. I was not trying to be *someone else*. I just wanted to be a better version of myself. I liked who I was before all the hurt and pain. I am still working on myself, and each day, I make a little more progress. I've come a long way, but as you all know, some old habits are hard to break.

I had done so much damage, and I'd been damaged goods for so long I didn't know where to start. It took some time for me to realize what I had to do. I had no closure from Ding Dong who hurt me until I ran into him eighteen years later (*I was already in a relationship at this point*). We talked and hashed everything out, and something very foreign came to me: all these feelings came back to me like I still wanted to be with him, like I still loved him, but I knew they were false. The more we talked, the more I felt I no longer hated him. In fact, from the conversations we had, I got complete closure, and I knew I was able to not think about him or the situation in which had control over me from that point forward. After I sat down and thought about the entire situation from how it all happened to where I was now, it devastated me at how I allowed him to have so much control over me all those years. We had not been in contact at all with each other for over eighteen years, and yet here I was giving him all this power. Ding Dong had no idea how I allowed him to have so much control over my life, which caused me to do what I had done.

When you get angry from what someone else has done to you and you allow that anger to sit still inside, you allow them to have power over you. They may not even know they have that power, but you give it to them. Don't allow someone to have that much control over your life; you lose precious time and energy and you can't get either of those back when you give them away.

He was still the same son of a bitch he was when we were younger. I, on the other hand, had changed into a woman to be reckoned with. Sexy lil ol' me was different in every way imaginable from the time we had been together. He wanted us to get back together, and it was my pleasure to let him know that it could **NEVER** happen. Most people would say I was the devil in a red dress, but in reality, I was the devil's mother covered in good looks, pain, hurt, and revenge; and I was mean. I kept my tail tucked and my horn covered so no one could see them. I was more than a force to be reckoned with; the devil had nothing on me!

Although I was in a relationship, talking to Ding Dong about the past and why what happened, happened, I knew with all my heart and soul I loved the person I was with more so now than before, but there was still a part of me (my brain was talking to me loudly) saying, "Let's keep doing what we've been doing and move on. No other man is supposed to have your heart. All he is going to do is damage you like Ding Dong did, and you won't be worth anything. You're not supposed to catch feelings; you are not supposed to fall in love. What is wrong with you? Get yourself together. Why would you want someone to have that much power over you again? You know damn well the man you love is going to cheat on you. That's what men do. They are dogs."

But my heart said, "If you don't sit down and take a moment to reflect on yourself and think about what you are about to do, you're not ever going to be happy. You say you want to love again. You say you miss how it feels to be in love. You want to be able to share a life with someone. How are you going to do that being a dog? How are you going to do that being such a deceitful temptress? How are you going to do that being so untrustworthy? How are you going to do that with no feelings, emotions or love in your heart? How are you going to do that with having no respect enough for yourself to stop doing what you are doing all together?" I had a fight going on within myself; this was a battle which was going to turn into a war of wars.

Clearly I had some soul-searching to do within myself. I was never going to be happy with a man until I fixed myself first. In the beginning, I could not see this. I had no idea about the road I was going to go down or what path I was going to travel. I had no idea it was going to be so hard for me to get back to being able to love. I was blinded by so much hate and destruction I was still a little furious and, most of all, I was scared to death and scared to love again; just the thought of it made me quiver. I thought I could just turn off the switch and be in a relationship.

Boy was I kidding myself. I was not going to be happy until I confronted all my issues. I was not going to be happy until I got some closure in my life. Also, I noticed with all I had done in the past, I was going to have issues with trusting. Trust is not something to be taken lightly; you have to earn trust. I was going to have a hard time because I had done so much wrong to so many others I knew karma was going to do me in. It's not that I had trust issues with my partner but trust issues within myself, thinking that eventually someone was going to do me the same way I did the men of my past. I figured, it was all going to come back and haunt me.

Let me point something out to you. I lived my life listening to my mind; if my mind said let him go, then that's exactly what I did. I did not want ANY man to get close to me. I wanted **NO** attachments to **NO ONE**! That helped me (*well, I thought it did*), and it did to a point. I had no idea I was so angry for so long; I had no idea I was self-destructing from the hurt I received from one man. I had no idea HE HELD SO MUCH POWER over my life until it was too late. My actions were affecting everyone (including myself), and I hadn't taken notice, and the notice that I did take I didn't care. I figured it was all well deserved because I figured, at some point in that man's life, he hurt a woman somewhere along the way before he met me. That's how I coped and how I rationalized what I was doing to these men. Not only that but I was also comfortable with hurting their feelings and putting them through an emotional state. It didn't matter to me if I was damaging them. I was the one that was scorned and hurt, so no one else mattered. (*It was all about me*). That was just selfishness on my part.

One day (years later), this guy and I ended up messing around, and one day, out of the blue, my heart spoke to me. Now, at this point, I was conflicted for the reason being my heart had been dormant and numb for all those years. When my heart spoke to me, it threw me off-balance and I was in the middle of a battle: *heart versus mind*. I wanted to put on my running shoes and go, so I put on my shoes and laced them up, but I couldn't move. I felt like I had concrete around my feet. At that moment, I knew it was time for me to take a stand, stop running, and settle down because the man I was with was the one for me!

I had dogged out so many men in my past—some I still talk to, others I don't. The one that broke my heart in the beginning wanted us to get back together, and all I could do was laugh at him. I was so tickled by that I laughed until I cried. I still have those who say they wish we could be together, but I think to myself, *You could never handle a woman like me*. But I don't say it 'cause, deep down inside, they know they can't. I made myself unobtainable to everyone I came across, and then there was him.

I have been in the relationship with the man I am with now for seven years. It has been anything but easy dealing with me and my issues. I have put him through a lot; there have been a lot of ups and downs, and there have been a lot of talks. This man knows more about me than any other man I've been with (*considering I did not want anyone to get close to me*). He may even know more about me than I know about myself. I've had a lot of work I needed to do, and I've had a lot to work on when it came to being in a relationship. I am still working on some of my issues, but the barriers that were holding me back (*to love*) I have crossed. I am now a new woman, and I have only changed the one and most important thing about me thus far—that being my heart, being able to love again is a reward all in itself! The past can no longer control me; the hurt no longer has control over my feelings. It feels good to love again; it feels good to be loved.

My life lessons, my struggles, my hurt, my pain, my actions, and all that I have been through is why I now can write this book. I have to say that being in love again has made so many positive changes in my life. The man I'm with has made me a better person. I love him more than any person I've ever loved before. The man I'm with has made me an honest woman (*never in a million years did I think that could happen*). He has changed me for the better, and he brings out the best in me; he has made me extremely happy. When someone says his name, my heart skips a beat, my face lights up, and an immediate smile goes on my face. No man has ever had that kind of effect on me. All I can say is, **IT FEELS SO GOOD TO BE IN LOVE AGAIN** and it's better than what I've experienced in the past.

Giving love another try was the best decision I've ever made in my life. To those of you who's going through tough times in your relationship right now, the best thing you can do is work it out (*if you want to be together*), talk through your situation, and understand what you both want. If you feel that you are not compatible, please, by all means, don't waste each other's time. Separate and move on. There is no time like the present to make changes and make things better. You can't change the past, but you can change the future for yourself. You are either going to accept the mistakes you and/or your partner have made and forgive each other and/or yourself and move forward, without holding a grudge or being spiteful. Or you are going to let each other go and move on with life. Time is precious, and no one needs to be where they don't want to be.

There is nothing better in life than knowing you have someone in your life that you know you can count on and who can count on you. When you have someone you love as much as you love yourself (*if not more*), then you will be the ultimate couple and plan on people being very envious of that! People will always try to ruin something that's good, so don't let people know your problems and what you're going through with your significant other. Fact is, people are jealous (whether they show it or not); they can/will use that to destroy everything that you've worked so hard for. People act like they are happy for you (and they seem to be happy themselves) but show a weakness in your relationship and watch how they will manipulate your circumstance.

I am not saying all of what I did was the thing to do, but I will say this: I enjoyed living outside of the box, beyond the boundaries, within the grasp of everyone else's opinions and judgments. What other people thought of me made no difference in my life, and I didn't lose any sleep over what the world thought of me. It did not bother me one bit. I only have one life to live, and I have to live my life as I see fit, no matter what is going on. I also learned quite a bit about life along the way. There are mountains, hills, valleys, roadblocks, potholes, and obstacles that have to be overcome, but you have to make the best decision for yourself in order to move—whatever direction that may be.

Enough about me. Let's move on with it. Now with that being said, enjoy what you read, and I hope you get a little something out of this book for you and yours, whether it be from my experience or an experience that you've been through or you're going through.

(*If you need to go back to square one and start all over again, this time before you get started, think about what you need to do in order to make yourself better and then proceed to move forward*).

Let's Take a Break

INTERMISSION 1

He said, "Come here, baby. I want to see if you taste as good as you look." She walks over to him, stands in front of him, wearing sexy blue lingerie, laced with sequence, a matching pair of blue crotch-less panties. She has on a pair of silver-and-blue platform peep-toe shoes with a pair of thigh-highs, which have a seam going down the back of her leg. She smells of pure ecstasy. Her legs are smooth as satin; the glow she has is as refreshing as pure oxygen. He says to her, "Stand in front of me." She pleases her king by standing in front of him; she walks over to him with a sexy, seductive walk. She stands in front of him with her legs slightly apart, holding a flogger. As she stands in front of her king, he gets up from the bed and he looks her in the eye and then leans over to her ear, grabs a handful of hair, pulls her hair and her head falls back, then says, "goddamn, you look sexy and smell like you need to be eaten alive. The way you look is turning me on."

He proceeds to kiss her on her neck, running his other hand down her back as he gets down to her ass; he grabs a handful, bringing her closer to him, and she feels the hardness of his manhood coming through his pants. He lets her go and tells her to get in front of the bed and bend over. She does as she is told, placing the flogger next to her on the bed. He steps in behind her, using his foot he spreads her legs apart just how he wants them. He unfastens his belt and unzips his pants, allowing his pants to drop to the floor. He is so hard that his manhood found its way out of the opening of his boxers. He drops to his knees, pulls her crotch less panties to the side and eats her out from behind. The warmness of his tongue against her cat causes her to get wet, and she moans from the feeling of the texture of his tongue. She grasps the sheets on the bed, moaning, while the sensations run through her entire body, causing her to flinch and quiver. He knees are getting weak, and her legs start to shake. He's sucking, licking, kissing, and sticking with his tongue. He stops oral and places two fingers inside her slowly, penetrating her, feeling her warmth and wetness on his fingers and how the cat is fitting around his finger, pulling them in like a vacuum. As he pulls his fingers out, he says to her, "You taste like candy and you're warm like a summer's night." He tells her to turn around; as she turns around, he tells her, "You are in for a night of immeasurable pleasure with your sexy ass."

She stands before him, noticing his erection; she grabs his erection in her hand, and he places his two fingers in her mouth, and she sucks her sweetness from his fingers. She goes to her knees to give him a taste of heaven, placing him inside her warm, wet mouth. She then begins to play with his balls while sucking his shaft, slowly filling her mouth with his manhood. She then pulls his manhood out and goes to sucking his balls while she plays with his manhood in her hand. Ooh, such a warm sensation goes through his body, and the way she is handling him, he's getting weak. His legs are starting to shake and give way; he wants to scream with pleasure because now she is sucking his manhood like she's hungry.

He said, "Mmm, ooohh, baby, wait, stop!" She stops, and he turns her around, and he walks them to the bed. He grabs her hair and pulls her head back; as she stands with her back toward him, he reaches his hand around the front of her body and places his two fingers inside of her, penetrating her, and feels the wetness running down his hand and says, "I see you ready for me, baby!"

He tells her to get in the doggy-style position on the edge of the bed. He grabs the flogger and places himself inside of her already warm wetness, knowing that it was all wet by him and ready for him. Her walls wrap ever so softly and tightly around him, like a glove fits its counterpart. It feels so good to him he spanks her with the flogger. That surprises her and stimulates her, sending a rush of emotion and sensation through her body, causing the warm fluids from her body to erupt a little more. She says, "Ooh, baby, that feels so good. Do it again." Since he is the one in command, he's not taking orders; he's giving orders. He strokes her slow and deep to make sure to enjoy the warmness and the sensation of her. It feels so good to her that she starts to stroke him back. She strokes him back with the same repetition he gives her. He grabs her hips and controls her movements.

He bends over and whispers in her ear, "I love the way you feel wrapped around me and how it pulls me back in." Then he pulls out and says to her, "Get up on the bed and lie on your back and spread your legs for me." She does as her master says to do; all the while he takes off his boxers, with readiness in his eyes, wanting her, desiring her. She looks back at him with intent, readiness, and the desire to feel him inside of her. He gets on the bed and looks her over with all his sexual desires built up in him; he's hard and ready to feel the wetness of her insides that they both have each other ready for. He hovers over her and starts to undress her with his teeth. This turns her on more, her panties come as he unties her lingerie with his teeth and her breast, so full and voluptuous, falling partly to the side, and he sucks on her nipples and plays with them with his tongue. She's exposed, and she looks ever so flawless. He goes back up and orders her to spread her legs open, and he licks her clit with his warm, wet tongue, making her moist; hearing her moan turns him on more. His mouth is wet and watering from the delicious taste of her. He continues to lick her from her clit to her breast, and he suckles on her nipples and makes his way to her neck as he rubs the hardness of his manhood up against her kitty cat.

He then grabs a ribbon and binds her hands together to the headboard. Her thigh-highs and her heels are still on. He looks over her body and then stares at her intently face-to-face and eye to eye. The buildup of all the sexual intentions, secretions, and readiness for each other is ready to explode in both of them. He mounts her and teases her with his manhood by only sticking in the tip and giving her short, slow strokes, suckling her neck and saying in her ear, "You ready for me, baby? You want all this inside of you? Show me how bad you want me without whispering a word." She then tries to grab him by his waist with her legs and pulls him inside of her, trying to pull him close to feel all his manhood inside. He watches her squiggle and squirm to try to get him to give way and let her feel him inside of her. He then pulls back and places her knees to her ears; while doing so, he looks her in the eyes and places in his manhood halfway inside her, and she gasps at just the feeling of him entering her, how he feels against her walls, and the way that he goes inside of her and fills up her walls. He places himself all the way inside her slowly, going deep; he feels her walls wrapped around him so softly, gripping him and pulling him inside. It feels so good to her that she moans, in ecstasy, all the tension and build up exists her body.

It's been over a week since she's seen him. As she sits with her legs crossed, trying not to think about him between them, she is fighting ever so hard the urge of her sexual gratification ever so quietly. As she sits at her desk at work, trying not to think about the satisfying sex they have every time their bodies collide with each other, her vagina begins to scream out to her ever so loudly how bad it needs to get its fix. It's like a crackhead who got high once and wants to hit the pipe again to get some kind of gratification even if it was just a little bit. Just to feel the tip going in then coming out slowly, just a little hit would make it ease up some of the madness it is creating between her legs. Her heart begins to race with thoughts of him touching her body. She can feel her temperature rising and every inch of his body on top of hers. She can feel his hands caressing her body as he breathes in her ear and then begins to suck on her neck, causing her to go into a rage of uncontrollable emotions. She wants to rape him as he sits and plays with herself between her legs. She wants to pull him in all the way so she can feel every inch of him inside her, causing her to rain and storm. The feel of him against her walls is ever so relishing; all the stress is being released and running from her body. The wanting of him inside of her causes her to palpitate. She wants him like wanting water after running a marathon in the desert.

She snaps back into reality and realizes she's at work, but the thought of him and the places it takes her makes her want him. Time to send him a text message!

You cannot change the past accept your
present self, you now have the power to make
you better for the present and future.

—L. Childs

A STRONG MARRIAGE REQUIRES LOVING YOUR
SPOUSE EVEN IN THOSE MOMENTS WHEN THEY
AREN'T BEING LOVEABLE; IT MEANS BELIEVING
WHEN THEY STRUGGLE TO BELIEVE IN THEMSELVES.

—DAVE WILLIS

Chapter 2

The Dilemma

He proposed to me. OMG, he proposed. We're getting married. I can't believe it. I love him so much; he's the best thing that ever happened to me. A girl couldn't have asked for more! I could not have asked for a better man. I am the luckiest girl in the world. He makes me happy, he listens to me, and he's there for me. I'm his yin to his yang. We have all the pieces of the puzzle put together; we are the perfect match. He's just perfect! So endearing, so loving! He's the best of the best, and he's all mine! I never thought I would have found the man of my dreams. It just seems too good to be true, but here we are, about to tie the knot, and he's all mine! I never thought this would happen to me, but it has and I am ready to take the plunge. He makes me feel like no other man has ever made me feel, and I couldn't ask for more.

* * *

Ten years later…

WHAT THE HELL DO YOU MEAN YOU'VE BEEN HAVING AN AFFAIR? WHAT THE…WHO IS SHE? HOW LONG HAS THIS BEEN GOING ON? HOW COULD YOU DO THIS TO OUR FAMILY? WHAT IS WRONG WITH YOU? YOU DON'T LOVE ME, YOU SELFISH INCONSIDERATE BASTARD. I CAN'T BELIEVE YOU. SO IN ESSENCE, YOU WEREN'T WORKING LATE, YOU

WEREN'T OUT AT THE BAR DRINKING WITH THE BOYS, YOU WERE OUT WITH SOME HOME-WRECKING WHORE. HOW COULD YOU? WHY, WHY, WHY DID YOU DO THIS TO ME, TO US? WHAT ABOUT THE CHILDREN? HOW DO YOU THINK THEY ARE GOING TO FEEL? HOW DO YOU THINK THIS IS GOING TO AFFECT THEM? I CAN'T BELIEVE THIS IS HAPPENING. HOW COULD YOU? YOU SELFISH SON OF A BITCH! HOW DID WE GET TO THIS POINT? WHY DID YOU LET IT GET TO THAT? YOU PUT OUR FAMILY IN A DILEMMA AND A TRAGEDY. NOW YOU'RE TELLING ME THAT YOU LOVE HER. GET THE FUCK OUT. I WANT A DIVORCE!

In the beginning, there was **undying love** for each other. There was **communication**—nothing that couldn't be talked about. There was **consideration** of each other's feelings and thoughts. Everything was done together which created a **bond** that was unbreakable. There was **loyalty** to each other. The **trust** that was built which didn't happen overnight; it was built through a rapport over **time**. The energy that went into making the relationship happen and work took a lot of time and effort on both your parts. There was nothing that either one of you could not talk about. There was no situation that you could not work through, but at some point, someone threw in the towel and called it quits. In any relationship or marriage, this can happen or has happened. Do we blame the person that cheated? Do we blame the actions that led up to the cheating? Do we blame the home wrecker? Do we blame the wife? Do we blame the husband? Who is to blame for this?

There are many reasons people cheat:

Feeling neglected at home (needs to feel wanted/sexy/appealing/ needed sexually).

A chance to explore different sexual varieties.

Curiosity.

No reason at all.

She or he might be motivated to have sex for reasons that have nothing to do with the personal relationship they are in when it occurs.

She or he feeling desired by another person.

She or he wants to try a new experience.

Want to harm their partner due to their partner cheating on them, wanting get back.

Getting back at an enemy (sleeping with the rival's partner).

In either instance (as far as cheating) this is going to cause a problem in any relationship and will lead to one or more people getting hurt emotionally, physically and mentally. This can and will provoke jealously in anyone.

I am no relationship expert by any means, but I believe I can say I've had my share of relationship issues, sexual struggles, heartache, and plenty of experience to say what I am going to tell you. Now what you need to also know about me is I am very much a lady in every aspect of the word, but I am also a tomboy. With both of these combined and the way I have navigated things (carry myself, dress, and act), I am very appealing not only to the eye but in conversation as well, especially with men! With my own self experiences aside, which are also going to play a part in what I am going to say in this book, I would like to open the door to another area and open your eyes to a few things. Hopefully you will learn a few things about yourself and your relationship and have a different outlook on life and a few other things along the way. Now as I said before, I am no expert but I consider myself as a person in which I can see things from a different spectrum, his side and her side. I have walked on both sides of the fence *(if you will)*. Let me see if I can open your eyes and your mind a bit on the issue.

Let me ask you a few questions:

1. Are you still doing the same things that you were doing when you first met?
2. Have you changed anything about yourself?
3. Do you know what you like?
4. Have you done anything at all differently?
5. Do you make time for the two of you?
6. Do you still think that what turns him/her on is the same as it was when you first met?
7. Is sex the same?
8. What have you done to change or make things better?

9. Have you talked to your significant other about your thoughts/fantasies?
10. Have you mentioned changes you would like to make?
11. Have you talked about what you would like to try?

As you get older, things in life change: your taste buds, your change in men/women, your age, your makeup. You move to another state/city (*change of scenery*), and you desire things that you never thought you would desire. You evolve over time; you think differently as maturity takes over. But nevertheless, we are still very curious, frisky, desirable, wanting, and needy creatures. I like to say that we grow up to fit in the workplace, but when we're out and we let our hair down, we act like teenagers. We act *youthful!* When acting in such a way, we have fun, we remember what is was like to be carefree, we laugh more, and we enjoy the company of others. We like entertaining and being entertained. It helps us to feel more alive, it relieves stress, and it also makes memories that we can look back on and laugh about. Now of course, since all that has changed, then you should know that sex has changed in a lot of aspects: what you like, what turns you on, how you like it, etc.

Let's get back to the story and why you are reading this book.

As in the instance with the story above, I would have to say that both parties are at fault on the issue of cheating. You're probably thinking, "How could both parties be at fault when the other party cheated?" Let me help you with that answer. Go back to the questions that were asked earlier. (*Are you still doing the same thing you were doing when you first met?*) What did you come up with? If you have not made any changes (*either one of you*), then how do you expect to keep your spouse happy? If everything else in your lives change, then why can't you make a few adjustments? Women cheat emotionally as for men they can have sex with a woman and not have any feelings toward that person. Well, guess what? Women can do the same thing! The reason I say that is, I've done it multiple times in my life. Some men are emotional creatures and some women are emotional creatures. Things can go both ways. They say all a man needs is a time and a place to cheat, and a woman needs a reason to cheat. This may be true, and sometimes there is nothing that can be done about it. There is something that we can do to help negate the issue to a point. Let's look at this from another angle. Now she has a reason to cheat. Is her cheating going to solve anything? Things will get progressively worse and then it's tit for tat. What then would be the point of having the relationship or being in the relationship? You might as well be single since you will be acting as such. Two wrongs don't make a right; you learned that as a child. I'm going to assume very strongly you have learned that as a child.

Okay, now let's take a time out for a minute.

As with the questions that have been listed above, if things are the same as they were ten years ago, then there is going to be cause for anyone to have issues in the relationship or cheat. I'm not saying it's okay to cheat, but when the odds are against the both of you, the weakest one is going to cave in first. Now mind you, you both are a reflection of each other (you are as one). Although cheating should not be an option in the relationship, there are many instances where cheating is the answer for some people. Cheating is actually not an option; it's a choice made at any instance (without thought of the other person), and it's a selfish thought nonetheless. You can't expect someone to keep doing the same exact thing over and over again and continuously be happy with the end result: man or woman. Maybe there were a few things that the home wrecker was doing that the wife would not do or the wife stopped doing. Maybe the wife is not giving up the "nectar" because she is too tired, has a headache, not in the mood, or simply for the reason that she is upset. Women, you CANNOT—and I repeat, you CANNOT—punish a man by taking away something from him such as yourself because you are upset/mad/angry at him. Also for the men, the same goes for you because men, in turn, can do the same thing as women. No one can call the kettle black; no one can do tit for tat. We all learned, as children, that two wrongs don't make a right. Why, oh why, do we play the games that we play? Because it's what we grow up learning to do, and it's fun.

As women, we have all sat down with our girls at some point or another and discussed sex, men, who's good, who's bad, who made us wet, who kept us wet, who's dick is what size, how they made us feel, people we have been with, who was the best sex person we have ever had because he did this, he did that. And ooohhhh, it felt so good. I liked it when he did this with his tongue and when he would put me in this position, how he made me have an orgasm. You get the point. We've all had that one guy that made us feel so good when it came to sex. Now ask yourself this: why did you and how did you get so comfortable and forget about all the fun you can have with sex? If you sit down and you talk about the memories of the one man that made you feel good, then why don't you try to incorporate those actions into your marriage/relationship and what you have now? It doesn't have to be exactly the same but something similar or it could be better. Why don't you think about how you come across to your spouse when you are both together? Are you doing anything different? Are you doing something to catch his attention? Are you still doing the same ol' same ol' you were a few years ago?

I know I don't like routine by any means. I lose interest quickly. Some of you may like routine and some of you may not. I would like for you to learn how to think outside the box. I hope what I am about to tell you will get you out of a routine, a habit or at least open your eyes to other options. Most of us fall into a routine and don't even realize it. When you do realize that you have fallen into a routine, it's when you have either gotten into an argument or you're just sitting and talking or maybe even just took the time to think about everything. However the case may be, you've fallen off the tracks, and it's time to get back on.

I am a lady, no doubt, but I also have tendencies as a man does when it comes to sex and conversation in the manner of how men think and how they react to a woman's response and her body language. If I am bored with you or you are not doing things right and I tell you but you refuse to do nothing about it, then guess what! I am on to the next end of discussion. I'd much rather let you go than to cheat (although it does not matter to me whether you let me go or not. If I tell you we are not together but you chose to see us as an item, then deal with what I do). But some men refuse to let the relationship end; then that's when, in turn, you have to find a way to let him/her down easy so you can move on. I don't know of any recipe to break things off with someone because every person is completely different when it comes to their feelings and emotions. Then you also have those that just can't let go (or refuse to let it go); those are usually the ones that are more invested mentally and don't want to see you with anyone else even if the relationship is unhealthy. When it comes to letting go or getting out of a relationship, both men and women can become obsessive with not letting the other partner "move on" as easily. They (in a manner of speaking) linger around, being in and out of your life. It can be hard to cut people off and out of your life, but you also have to be strong enough and willing to do it, especially when it's unhealthy.

If I tell you that things are just not good and you don't want to up the game, then bye-bye, baby. You need to go and I have to move on. If something is said about a situation and you are willing to make necessary changes and sacrifices for the betterment of the relationship but your partner is not, well then, sad to say, things need to end. You have to be able to keep things interesting at all times. Doing something different and out of the pocket keeps the sex life exciting and leaves you wanting for more and stepping out of your realm to try something else. Nothing is better than thinking about your significant other all day while you are at work because of what happened the other night. Here you are, walking around the office all day with a glow and smile on your face because your significant other put it there.

When you are in a relationship and you have a partner you are either married to or want to marry, you have to keep everything interesting. Not start it one way and then let it all fall off. So many times we do what's needed to start the relationship in the beginning, and then we all get lazy and let everything fall into the crack of life. Once the fire is started in the beginning you have to keep it going throughout. Yes, I know this is not an easy task to do and neither is life. Things are not always fair in the relationship and things are not always fair in life. But people will make time for what they want to make time for. People will make sacrifices for what they want to make sacrifices for. So why should the sex life be any different?

What are the elements that construct a relationship you ask? Let's get to that.

The BUILDING BLOCK foundation of a relationship stems from the following:

✓ Time   ✓ Loyalty
✓ Trust   ✓ Love
✓ Communication   ✓ Sex
✓ Work

Maybe not necessarily in that order but let's go with it for now; all relationships start differently. When you put time into someone, you are building trust, and in order to build trust, you have to communicate, and in order to communicate, you have to work at it. You also start building up loyalty to each other and then you start to involve emotions (*love*), and then there is the sex which intertwines the both of you together and builds an emotional bond.

Now if you build your relationship alone off sex, well, then don't expect to be in that relationship long. That's more of a fly-by-night sex partner where the sex can be good and, yes, you have communicated to an extent, i.e., what time, where, and how long we got. You are not taking time to build a rapport nor are you trying to get to know each other, but since the sex is oh so good, I want to be with you. That is not about to happen due to the fact you only know each other sexually and haven't taken the time out to know each other personally. You will find that there are things about a person that you don't like at all and can't live with even though the sex is fantastic. We all have our quirks and what we think makes a relationship strong.

Let's start from the beginning. Now what did you do to get your spouse? Once you start something, you can't stop doing that; maybe you can change things up a bit, but you can't completely stop doing something altogether and think that everything is copacetic. When you were courting each other, you took time out to figure out which outfit you were going to wear, you sat there and tried to figure out what to do with your hair, and you might have even gone as far as getting a manicure and a pedicure. You took a shower or soaked in the tub for a few, put on some nice lotion, body spray, or parfume (*you know the one that smells the best on you*), put your outfit (*after trying about ten of them*), looked yourself over and over and over and a few more times to make sure everything was in place. Then you went out on your date, and you both had a good time and did it a few more times. You dated for a while, and then all of a sudden, he popped the question and you said yes.

After marriage and a few years of being married, you both stopped doing all that. You get comfortable and you've established a pattern; you may not notice but you have. You both know what to expect of each other; in essence, you have a schedule to follow. You both got stuck in the *American lifestyle* as I like to call it. Get the man/woman, get married, have children, and the relationship goes to being blah. The sex is on an if-I-feel-like-it basis or if we both are in the mood, but it's not good sex; you're just going through the motions of sex. Now what fun is that?

All this plays a part in your relationship, and over time it gets dull, boring, and repetitive; and eventually, one or both of you lose interest in each other due to the fact that neither of you are paying attention to the other. The time you took to build the relationship has come to a complete halt. The trust is now a thin line (husband or wife working late, going out to the bar to have a few drinks, coming home in a stupor). All the communication is short, if any at all. The work that you put into the relationship to build it and keep it together is nonchalant. In some sense of the word, you both have gone your separate ways, but you are still married. The loyalty is no longer a factor. The love is turning more into irritation, irrationality, and anger. Neither of you are doing anything about it. You try to cover it up and make it seem like things are fine, and all you are doing is trying fool yourself. The sex, well, that became more of a job and not worth doing; neither one of you like it. Now what do you do? What made you feel the way you feel? Time to take a step back and look at the entire picture and observe what's going on.

Ladies, ladies, ladies. I just might take you by surprise when I say what I am going to say. By all means, don't take what I am going to tell you the wrong way. YOU are going to LEARN something about yourself TODAY! I'm not telling you this just to keep or save your relationship. I am telling you this for the reason being, I want all of you, ladies, to bring sexy back to your life. I want you to be able to feel confident, put that stride back into your walk, be sexy, feel sexy, be seductive, sensual, be the temptress that you are, and be the cat on the prowl, and purr, baby, purr.

What I want you to understand is how to connect and be in tune with yourself. Once you get in tune and connect with yourself, imagine how you are going to feel, imagine what is going to change, and just imagine what you are going to do to your spouse! We have all spent plenty of time with ourselves alone. Sometimes we sit around the house bored with nothing to do. There are times where we get horny and feel the need to have sex, but your partner is not around to fill that wanting and urging need.

If you need to put on some sexy music, pop in a porn and have some me time. Clear your mind and relax for a bit. There is nothing wrong with getting a lil horny; you have yourself to deal with, and no one else is there but you.

A man loves a woman that knows what she wants and how she wants it even if that means she has to show him. What does that mean? We will talk about that later in this chapter. Now I know we've all had sex or made love, so none of us are new to sex! At some point in life, we have established what we like when it comes to sex. There is a difference between what we like, how we like it, and having "military sex" as I like to call it. That military sex is the sex movements on the command of the spouse; there is no fun in that. Now when it comes to BDSM, that is something different and, for some, very enjoyable. But don't put BDSM down, especially if you have not experienced any part of it. Don't knock it till you try it. DBSM is not just about the bondage and the spanking. There's so much more to it than what you think. Have you ever been tied to the bed and blind folded and drizzled with chocolate and whipped cream while your significant other licked it off of you with his tongue and teased you while he did it? That is part of BDSM.

You should be as one or at least be able to know what is going to happen when you are with your spouse. You also can take your spouse/significant other by surprise (*if they like surprises*). You know when your man is about to change positions, you know when he wants to pick you up; there are little cues or hints that you give each other, and sometimes you both just roll with the flow.

Marcus Houston has a song titled "Swag Sex." Ladies, you better put a lil swag in your sex; it's not just him, it's you as well. You have to remember the shoe fits both ways. You have to know that you can lay it on your husband/significant other so good that all he can think about when he goes to work on Monday (*or whatever day he goes to work*) is the awesome weekend/night that he had with his wife/woman. It will be like a movie playing over in his head, and he is going to think about it all day. He may even shoot you a text or two, telling you how he enjoyed last night's or this morning's sex. He will be ready to come back home after work to see you again. You should always make sure that you give him something to remember when he leaves the house. I am not saying you have to do this every day, but when you do, do it and make sure you make it memorable. Everything that you do, do it well. You should make a lasting impression always! You will also make it memorable for yourself; you may even surprise YOU. If there is nothing better than what a man likes, it's studying his woman's anatomy in every aspect of the sense.

You want to know how to do this? You want to know the process to do this? You want to know how much this is going to cost you? (Well, it cost you this book, so get ready.) Do you want to know how to keep him happy? I'm sure you want to also keep yourself happy and satisfied. It's not just about him; it's about you too. There is nothing better than to have the fire you once had for each other. There is nothing better than connecting back with the one you fell in love with. You both want to be able to keep each other happy in every way imaginable. You've both have gotten out of sync with one another and seem to be going down different roads. Please remember to keep an open mind. You have to pay close attention in order for this to work. First, let's get the basics out of the way. Let's see what it is that my husband/significant other likes:

1. *What arouses his senses—i.e., vanilla, cinnamon, berries? If they are candles, light them; if it's a scent you wear, put it on, etc.*
2. *What's his favorite position?*
3. *What does he like to see you in? Wear it.*
4. *What turns him on about you? Emphasize that.*
5. *What does he like to see you do—i.e., private dance, cook naked, walk in heels?*
6. *How does he like to be touched? Touch him there in a sensual way.*
7. *What is his favorite color? Incorporate that in what you wear or in the room before you rock his world.*
8. *Does he have a favorite football/basketball/hockey team? Time to dress up and role-play.*
9. *Does he like to see you in heels? Put on a pair.*
10. *Does he like a particular room in the house? Time to set up your evening there.*
11. *Does he like for you to call him pet names—i.e. daddy, baby, beast, monster?*

What you are doing here is creating an environment for him. Actually, it's for the both of you. Let's go back and look. You are taking time out to appeal to your man's needs. You already know how to answer all the questions about him: his likes about you, his favorite color, and a few other characteristics that you can incorporate to a night with him. All you have to do is apply that to pleasing him. You have to appeal to your man, as I like to call my man king.

"Ohh, baby, yes, that, mmmm, ohhh, give it to me." This will help him and feed his ego. Don't ever be afraid to talk to your man while you are in the middle of making love/having sex. You, as his queen, are supposed to feed his ego and let him know that he's the man, the one and only, the alpha, the king of the fortress. Every man likes to feel and know that he is the king of your fortress—your body.

He likes to know that he is in control and what he has you love it, not like it. LOVE IT! Every woman is supposed to blow her man's head up especially when it comes to lovemaking/sex. There is NOTHING wrong with stroking your man's ego; you have to let him know that he is, in fact, the KING of your domain. You have to let him know that he is the one. You have to build your man up, build his confidence, build up his manhood (talk about how good it feels to you), and look at him like you look at no other. You are each other's jungle; there's a lot of exploring and new territory to find on each other. Getting reacquainted can be so much fun and entertaining for the both of you.

Ladies, I know you might not want to hear this after you have worked all day and got home and cooked dinner and took care of the kids, etc., but you also have to take care of your man. Listen, a woman's work is NEVER done. But also know that this works the other way around too, gentlemen. Your woman needs to be taken care of as well; you cannot neglect each other. If she comes home from work and she has dinner cooked and the house is tidied up (*I say that 'cause working/kids/cooking is a lot of work during the week*), then, men, you can pitch in to help ease some of the burden. Wash the dishes, do a load of laundry, sweep and mop the floor, vacuum, rub her feet, do something to help ease the load. If she is in the kitchen cooking dinner, why don't you offer her some help with washing the dishes that are in the sink? She is your queen, so you need to treat her as such! You can't expect a woman to be at your beck and call and treat you like a king when you, in turn, don't want to treat her like the queen she is. A man that helps a woman around the house is sexy whether you believe it or not.

Do something a little different, like role-play. Act like you are going on a blind date and meet each other somewhere and let him use his pickup lines on you. Role-play in the bedroom: cops and robbers, Indian and chief, burglary, babysitter, it does not matter, but let's get some kind of action going on in the bedroom to spice it up! If you can turn up with your girls and if you can turn up with your boys on the weekend, then you should be able to turn up, turn out, and show out for your spouse. That's when it's time to show your seductive side and give him/her everything you got. If your man travels a lot, there is nothing wrong with some FaceTime phone sex. Even if he does not travel and he is just away from the house for a certain time, that could be in the middle of the afternoon while he/she is at work. You have to build up some anticipation because when he/she comes home, you already know what is going to happen. Get it spicy and keep it that way. Nothing wrong with some anticipation in the relationship, nothing wrong with being freaky, nothing wrong with breaking out of the shell, nothing wrong with thinking out of the box, and absolutely nothing wrong with pleasing and teasing each other. That makes for an explosive night!

Couples who make it aren't the ones
who never had a reason to get divorced:
they are simply the ones who decided
early on that their commitment to each
other was always going to be bigger
than their differences and flaws.

—Dave Willis

Chapter 3

Time

Time

noun \'tīm\: the thing that is measured as seconds, minutes, hours, days, years, etc.

Time stops for no one, and the clock is ticking. What are you doing with the time that you have now? You never know how much time you have to do the things you need to do. You are never promised time. You don't want to waste your time. You don't want to waste someone else's time. Don't put off what you can do today for tomorrow.

Time is a very important factor in life no matter what it is you're doing. To me, it's one of the most important factors, reason being that you never know how much time you have. You never know if you will have the opportunity to tell your spouse how much you love them; you never know if you will have time to apologize. Most of us think that time can get away from us (in days, weeks, months, and years), but not in the moment. Your life is built on time. How are you going to utilize something so precious?

Look at all the time that has passed from your childhood up until this very point. Look at what you have accomplished and look at the things that you have learned and gained and all the many things that you have been taught along the way. You learn something every day either about yourself or about life in general and what is going on around the world. Did you write down goals that you want(ed) to accomplish by a certain age? Did you accomplish those goals? If not, why? TIME! Some of us know how to manage our time and others are horrible at managing time.

If you have never learned anything in your life, you learned that time is very valuable: it doesn't stop for anyone, it keeps going, time can heal wounds, time flies by when you're having fun. Remember how you were in a rush to grow up when you were younger because of all the rules and regulations that your parent(s) had? Now you've come to a point where you wish you could go back and do it all over again and change a few events in your life. There is either too many hours in a day or not enough hours in a day, you can't change anything that has happened in the past, but you can change the outcome of the future.

This is what you first started doing when you were getting to know each other. You spent quality time, you got to know each other's habits, dreams and goals in life, favorite color, likes, dislikes, weaknesses, strengths, families (distant and close). You got to know each other's favorite song (types of music each other likes) and behaviors. Believe it or not, all this getting to know each other is a big part of your life and time.

Time is very valuable especially when you spend it with someone else. This is one of the most important parts of your life that you give someone: TIME. You may not look at it as such a big factor, but have you ever said, "I don't know why I wasted so much time trying to help, talk to, stress over, or look out for this person when all they did was take advantage of me or use me"? All that took a part of time out of your life, and you can't get that time back. You sit back and reflect on what you could have been doing with that time.

This is what happens when you start dating:

In the beginning, you took time out to get ready, you made sure you looked good enough to eat, you made sure you smelled good, you made sure your hair was in place, etc. If you were the one making plans, you made sure you had everything organized, i.e., dinner reservations, a movie, a play, bowling, picnic, festivities, etc. All these things took time out of your day to get accomplished.

Is the person you are spending time with really worth your time? Are you being considerate of your own time? You can never get time back. You actually don't take all this into consideration before you do what you do; you just don't even know it. It takes time and patience to get to know someone. You not only get to know them but you also get close. You either go your separate ways because it's not going to work out, become friends, or become partners. Only time can decide the outcome of either of these factors.

Utilize your time wisely. If you and your spouse need to get to know each other all over again, then you both need to make TIME for it. Don't let time slip away from you! Make a list of things that you miss, like, dislike, and about how you feel about your spouse. Make a date, and don't be late. Rediscover each other if you need to, talk about everything on your list, make sure you LISTEN to each other. Most of the time, we hear each other, but we don't listen to each other when we're talking. Make sure that you are listening, and if there is something you don't understand, regurgitate what you heard and talk about it until you get an understanding. You have to be on the same page when it comes to communication. Everything has to be rationalized. Don't argue; I know this can be hard to do at times, but you have to learn how to listen—not yell, not scream, and both of you can't talk at the same time. If you both are talking at the same time, that means no one is listening.

Did you know that you don't get anything accomplished by yelling at each other? Surprise, surprise! You don't get anything accomplished by not resolving the issue at hand (ignoring the problem). All you have to do is calm down and take some deep breaths. If that means that you have to leave and walk around the block, then do so. If that means you have to go into the next room and have a moment to yourself, then do so, and your spouse should also allow you that s-p-a-c-e. When you come back, you can assess the problem at hand. After which, you can decide if it's just something that is temporary and an annoyance, or is it something that is more of a grievance?

You have to let each other know that you still care and you both still love each other. There is nothing more seductive to a woman's ears than to hear her man say, "I love you." You also have to know that the problems you have been dealing with is NOT more valued than your relationship. When you have come as far as you have, you can't just let the marriage or relationship go down the drain. You have to let each other know that you still have each other's best interest at hand. You can't just put all those years into each other, and then when one little simple thing comes along, you let it ruin the both of you. Fact of the matter is, when something useless comes along and you let it destroy all that you have, then neither one of you wanted it in the first place.

You have to let your queen know you have her back, and, ladies, you have to let your king know you have his back. It is so easy to give up and get a divorce, but when you get married, you made a solid proclamation with God and with each other (for better or worse, for richer or poorer). Words mean something, and you not only said those words, but you also took an oath in front of God. Those words have meaning to them, and they were not just for you to recite like you were reading them out of a science book or rehearsing a song. Words have meaning, and most people don't think about the meaning of words when they speak them. Take time out to think before you speak because you might regret what you say later. Always take into consideration the feelings of your partner before you speak. Don't speak out of rage or anger. Yes, I know this is easier said than done, but it's possible.

You may think, well, we're just going to give up and call it quits. Are you going to give up that easily? Is it that easy for you? Let me veer off here for just a minute and say this:

Did you fall out of love and make that a conscious decision based on how you feel at that very moment, or did you take time and come up with such a culmination? So many times have we said things out of anger or hurtfulness because we are in an argument, not at all thinking things through. All you want to do when you're arguing is hurt each other's feelings, and for what? Gratification for yourself to make it seem like you are the bigger person, to make it seem like you can remember all the details of the other person's wrongdoings or the mistakes they made, the fact that you can throw something back up in their face for what you did for them, even the small fact that you might have a bigger vocabulary than your significant other, the fact you may make more money than he/she does. It only makes you look like a fool when you try to demean your significant other because if you look at the entire situation, you are the one with him/her. Arguing does not fix anything, and a couple weeks or months down the line you are not going to remember what the argument was about in the first place. So re-evaluate what's at hand first. I know there are going to be disagreements and you are not always going to see eye to eye, which is healthy. But make sure you take time out to see each other's point of views. Stay calm and learn how to listen and hear one another out.

Now let's get back to the subject at hand.

Take this for instance. Let's say that someone broke into your house and one of you got hurt. You call the police, they come to the house. They show up to your door and the burglar got away. The police make a report and tell you they'll keep an eye out for the guy. Now let's say this happened a couple more times. Now it happens one more time, and the police tell you on the phone that they are not coming out to check on you because they are going to get the same end results they got before, but this time, the burglar is still in the house and one of you end up getting hurt terribly and sent to the hospital to be put on life support. The police decided to quit coming out because they figured the outcome would be the same; and they wanted to save themselves time, taxpayers' money, paperwork, and gas and continue to do whatever it was they were doing. That would piss you off for the simple fact you see how your tax dollars are being spent and you see how the "protect and serve" is at their leisure. That leads me to ask you this: are you in your marriage or relationship just for leisure and to pass time? What are you in it for?

You can analyze the problem and issues at hand with a clear mind and resolve the issue together. How much time do you get to spend together? How much time do you get to spend apart? What do you do with your time away from each other? Are you utilizing your time to the best of your ability?

Let me veer off here for a moment. Ladies, I need to talk to you on another level for a moment.

I am not trying to sound offensive. I am not trying to come across in a disrespectful way at all. Let me ask you this, how well do you know yourself? How much time have you spent understanding yourself? How much time have you spent analyzing your body? How much time have you spent looking at your own facial expressions? How about the way you move? Do you know what you look like when you do certain things? Do you know what is most sexy about yourself?

I know for myself that my form of communication is my facial expressions. It's so natural for me to make some kind of facial expression at some point during a conversation. I don't realize I am making these facial expressions because it's so natural for me to do it. It's just in my nature, whether good or bad. But I do know I make some kind of expression. I know how I walk. I know how I move. I know what my facial expression looks like when someone sees me for the first time or the hundredth time. I know what my body looks like naked and clothed. I know how my body feels. I know how I smell. I know how I taste. I know how I look in outfits. I know what I look like when I dance. I know what I look like when I'm intoxicated. I know what I look like when I am about to have an orgasm.

Ladies, you have to take some time and examine your own self inside and out. Do you feel sexy in your own skin? If not, why? You should know your faults; you should know more about yourself than anyone. In order for you to feel sexy and be in touch with your inner goddess (as I like to call it), then you should know yourself inside and out. You have to know what turns you on; you need to know what you like and dislike. There is nothing wrong with embracing yourself if only for just a moment. You need to get that goddess in you out. You need to know what buttons you push to get you in the mood. You need to learn how to talk dirty to yourself even if it's in third-party format. No matter the case, you are dealing with you and only you. Maybe you just need to rediscover who you are. Maybe you need to learn how to take a time out and redefine who you are. Maybe you need to rethink about how much fun you used to have. Maybe you really don't know who you are sexually.

The goddess needs to flaunt around every once in a while (or as often as needed); she has to let her hair down and become the prowess and purr like the cat she is. That's that alter ego, ready to be who she is. She wants to take control at some point. She wants to be free. She wants to have fun with no string attached. She wants to be sexy, fun, coddled, exposed, and embraced for who she is. She wants to be let completely loose and take complete control. That is something that you need to let her do, or it is going to drive you crazy. If you have never let the cat out of the bag, then you need to go ahead and let loose. It is going to make you feel so much better. You are going to do things differently in life, and changes are going to be made. Trust me when I tell you that when these changes are made, your significant other is going to notice and your significant other is going to very much like it. Stop being shy. You can also ask your partner what (s)he likes or would like to see you do. You know the kind of touch you like. You know how you like your husband/significant other to kiss you. You know how you like your husband/significant other to make you feel. Do you know how to make you feel like that too? You can surprise yourself with what you can find out when you spend time to get to know yourself. Do you know what you smell like? Do you know what you taste like? What's wrong with touching yourself? What is there to be embarrassed about? You are going to be with you; no one is going to be there with you. You are on a self-discovery time.

The point of this is for you to get to know you and your boundaries. Nothing wrong with that at all. You should be able to make yourself feel sexy, maybe not as sexy as your king can but close enough to it. You can at least find out what it is that you like and how you liked to be touched.

Before you get started, you should put on something that makes you feel sexy, get ready like you were getting ready for your husband/significant other. Turn on some lovemaking music (*or whatever kind of music puts you in the mood*). Look yourself over in the mirror. Model a little bit to see how you look. Flaunt and prance around in the mirror, dance, look at yourself in a different light. Just how sexy can you be?

You have to try something new for yourself. You have to love yourself from the inside out. When you love you, then others can love you for who you are. You have to respect yourself, and others will respect you. If they don't, then don't shed a tear. You have to be able to feel confident at all times whether you are at home alone or if you are out with others.

You are in control of you. You are in control of your feelings. Don't try to be that "other woman"; be your own woman and express all you have. Be bold, be outstanding, be courageous, be amazing in everything you do from this point forward. You are a sexy woman, and you need to fix that crown because it's crooked.

Now while you are doing that, prance around as if your husband/significant other where there with you or do it like no one is watching. All you have to do is let your mind be clear and think of things that are sexy and be at peace. Now touch yourself like you want to be touched. Pretty soon you will put yourself in another realm. You are on a self-discovery zone. You need to be in touch and in tune with yourself. You and your inner goddess need to be in tune with each other. Your inner goddess is ready to let loose and have some fun. When you let that goddess out of you, she will take control. If you need a little solace, then grab a glass of wine or two and get up some liquid courage to do this, if need be.

You can talk dirty out loud (if you were shy before). You can let out those sounds that you were too scared to let out before. There are things that you are going to discover about you that you didn't know. Thoughts may flood your mind that you never thought you would have thought before. You are about to find out a little something about you that even you didn't know. There is nothing like feeling sexy within yourself.

Your inner goddess has been screaming to come out and let her hair down. She likes to show off her body. She misses looking at herself in the mirror and prancing around. She loves to strut around and prance. She needs to come out and prowl from time to time. She misses showing out. She misses having that control in the bedroom.

That inner goddess is what makes you sexy. You have to bring the sexy back out of yourself. Once you get her out and you have learned yourself, you can then apply that to the life of you and your husband/ significant other.

There is nothing sexier than a man coming home from work and the house is dim with candles lit up all over the house (or the lights on low). Dinner on the table with a beer or wine (whatever he likes to drink). Some nice sexy mellow music and a sexy queen standing there in lingerie and heels, waiting for him to walk in the door so she can get him to the table and feed him. When he's done eating (if he can make it through the presentation), he can get a little private dance to a song which is going to turn up the heat in the room. You can show him to the couch and give your king a lap dance as you slowly reveal to him your skin and nakedness. He is going to be in awe of his queen. By the time the song is over, you should be in your birthday suit with a pair of heels on.

Now, men, this goes for you also. You can do something sexy for your queen as well. She does not always have to be the one doing something for you. A relationship works both ways; it's give and take, not just take. This is a good time for show and tell between the both of you.

Ladies, now that you know how to make yourself feel good, you know how you look when you are strutting across the room in those heels. You know how you look when you lie down. You know YOU! Now this is the time where you can let your husband/significant learn about you all over again, or this is your time to teach him what you like or learned about yourself. He is going to like learning. He is going to like pleasing that egotistical goddess you let out. Show him how you want to be sucked, touched, grabbed, spanked, tossed, hair pulled. Let him know how you want him to make you feel. Talk dirty to him; make him feel you.

It's time to step outside the box. It's time to open up and experiment. It's time to take a chance to venture out of your little boxed-in world. It's time to stop thinking what if and start doing, taking action. It's time to open the realm of your fantasies and make them happen. It's time to just do the things you've imagined. It's time to do the naughty things you've thought of. Let your king really see what you are made of. If you both want, you can go to a sex store and get things such as Kama Sutra and games the two of you can play together. What I like about games is that you can find out things about each other as you play them. You can find spots on each other that turn each other on that you yourself or your spouse didn't even know existed. It's like a form of foreplay, a little more intensified! You will both be turned on and ready to pounce on each other, which may even lead to conversations afterward about other things to do or try. Nothing wrong with going to the store to grab a flogger, spreader bar, oil, candles (for the wax), clamps, body butter, cuffs, dildo(s), ben wah balls, games, etc. You should be exploring with each other, trying out different things and positions. You learn something new every day, so don't stop with the sex. Learn more about sex. Invigorate yourself and then invigorate each other.

THE MOST SACRED PROMISE WE CAN EVER MAKE IS
THE PROMISE WE MAKE TO GOD AND OUR SPOUSE
ON OUR WEDDING DAY. IF THE WEDDING VOWS
DON'T MATTER, THEN NO PROMISE MATTERS.

—DAVE WILLIS

Chapter 4

Trust

trust
noun\ˈtrəst\
: belief that someone or something is reliable, good, honest, effective, etc.
: an arrangement in which someone's property or money is legally held or managed by someone else or by an organization (such as a bank) for usually a set period of time
: an organization that results from the creation of a trust

We all know this is a big four-letter word, and most people have issues with this alone. Trust has always been a big issue for me. Not because I don't trust who I'm with. I have trust issues with myself due to all of the wrongs I've done to the men which have crossed my path. I felt like the one man I give my all to is going to hurt the hell out of me, but at the same time, I can't keep holding myself back from what I most desire. I have insecurities I am still dealing with to this day, and the only way I'm going to get over that is to move on, let go, and proceed with life, meaning, letting myself be gullible and giving it another shot. I know I have to give him the benefit of the doubt and not let my thoughts overpower me. The problem I have is thinking that every man is the same. He is going to cheat; he is lying about this and that. He is talking to his friends about me and what we do.

It is hard to not categorize men to be the same when you have been in a bad relationship. When you have someone that is good, that is going to stick by your side, and be there for you no matter what, it's almost hard to fathom. You don't think it's real you keep doubts, and you look for reason to snoop around to see if he's doing what the other men did to you. Then you end up pushing him away when all he was trying to do was be good to you and show you that all men are not the same.

That is a very hard obstacle to overcome, but it can be done over time. It's all about building trust and communicating with one another about how you really feel.

Sometimes I have a hard time not thinking about my past, and it keeps coming back to haunt me. Though I have changed a lot about myself by giving love a second chance, I still have yet to overcome my fear of trust. Talking about it and doing it are two diversified worlds apart. The only way for me to get over it is to just let it go and have faith in the man I'm with. There is no other way around it. I don't care how you look at it. I have never had a problem with trusting myself, and I also have to trust my own judgment when it comes to trusting someone else.

I have been accused by so many men of cheating (even when I'm not) and it is the most annoying thing to deal with. Accusations can and will cause problems in any relationship. If you want to know something, just ask never be afraid to ask. If you continue to make accusations about the person, then you are asking for trouble in the long run. It's irritating to no end and also you may cause the person to go and do whatever it is that you are accusing them of. Be careful of what you say and how you say it.

The only thing I have done to help myself is talk myself out of my issues I have within myself. We can all either talk ourselves into something or talk ourselves out of something. It's all a matter of the mind. I still fight with myself on a day-to-day basis for different reasons (*we all have something we fight with*). Trust is not an easy obstacle to overcome; it doesn't matter if someone betrayed your trust or if you yourself have trust issues. Trust is an issue which is a matter of the heart no matter how the issue came about. When you have been betrayed, it hurts like hell and the only thing that can heal that is time, and everyone has their own healing process. Time is very precious, so you can't allow something take up too much of your time. If you are having a hard time dealing with any issue, you need to talk to someone about it, get a book and read about how you can help yourself, or go see a counselor.

Most of us have all been betrayed at some point in our lives, and sometimes that's hard to get over. When it comes to being in a relationship, trust is something that needs to be there. Trust is the biggest factor in any relationship. If you're with someone and you don't trust them, then why are you in the relationship? Why put yourself through heartache and pain? Why waste time? It only causes arguments and distracts your mind. There's no need for punishment, distraction, or anger for either one of you. What I mean by punishment is that there is no need to punish your significant other in view of the fact that you're insecure, not trusting enough or have/having second thoughts about him/her. You can't punish someone for someone else's mistakes. I know it's like me calling the kettle black or catch 22 in view of what I did (in the beginning). In my own selfish defense, I'm going to say this: I was young, inexperienced, I was not thinking about time and how this was going to affect me in the long run. I thought I had all the time in the world, and I knew what I was going through at that moment in time would be fixed in no time at all. So at least I thought! I can tell you now, it taught me a lot and developed me into the woman I am today, but it sure did take up a lot of my time and life.

Life and time teaches you all the lessons you need to know about life period. Life has a way of pointing things out later in time so you can see and learn from all your mistakes, downfalls, and triumphs. Experience is the best teacher, but if you have a willingness to learn and listen to the wise, that will make a huge impact on your life and make it better for yourself. You learn something new every day no matter who it's from; it could be from someone as simple as a toddler.

Betrayal has a couple of parts to it: verbal and nonverbal, also resulting in damage to one or both of the parties at hand. You always have to take accountability for your OWN actions; don't shift the blame. We, as humans, don't like to take responsibility for our own actions when we have either made a bad judgment call or when we've made a mistake. Trust and honesty go hand in hand. The reason I put own in all caps is due to the nature of people. NO ONE likes to look at what they have done to get the outcome they received from the other party. Some people like to always play the victim (man/woman) when something goes array. People like that are just looking for a way out; they are not looking to fix any problems that may arise or have arisen. Don't play the victim role. Take responsibility of your actions and your part at all times no matter if you did something stupid or uncalled for. Stand up and be a wo(man) about the situation.

Remember, the grass is not greener on the other side; it's just merely a mirage to get you to look in that direction. If the grass looks better to you and you cross that barrier, then you are in for a world of trouble to follow. Everything new looks good at first glance; it even looks good after you been checking it out for a while. When you decide that you want to get a new TV, you go to the store and talk to a salesman about it. The only reason you've gone to the store is because you were price shopping online and found they have the TV you want, but before you purchase it, you inquire about it. You ask all kinds of questions to see if this TV is going to fit your needs. Then you are going to take some time to make your final decision. Before you make your decision, you are going to go home, maybe do some more research first, and talk to your significant other about it, not to mention the warranty cost and repair cost in case something goes wrong. Things start to add up quickly, and the cost of the TV is not the same.

The only way to know which egg you have is going to take TIME to figure out, and who has time to waste like that? What you need to realize is, people are like eggs; you don't know what you're going to get until you crack it open, and that's when all the smell and crap is going to come out of it. Then and only then are you going to take a step back and realize what you have gotten yourself into.

The grass may look more appealing to you, but you don't know what the maintenance is going to cost or what it's like. People can keep up a facade about themselves for a long time to make sure they get what they can get out of you. Everyone has an angle of some kind no matter what it is and you can't always see which angle they're coming from. You have to think of men and women as wolves in sheep's clothing at all times.

There are people out there that are great at fooling you about who they are and what their angle is. Take me as a prime example.

There are people that are out here to make others miserable when they are happy. There are people out here jealous of what you have and/or who you're with. You've heard the saying, misery loves company. There are people out there handing out STDs like candy; some do it intentionally in view of the fact that they feel as though the person they were with should have told them they had XYZ disease, which could possibly kill them. Instead of them taking precautions of their own, they had to suffer the consequences of their own actions as well as the actions of the one they were with. There are people out here which want to break up a happy home. You have to make the choice of what it is you are going to do. You can't always see things at first, but you will in due time, and hopefully it will not become an option for you.

Now these are the options you have: you are either going to take the plunge and go to the other side and play for the other team or you are going to go back home and work with the team you already have. You are going to have to go and find the old playbook, draw up some new plays, and put things back in order. Always remember the other team is not YOUR team; they're out to make you lose, and if you don't have enough courage to fight draft season, then you're going to lose no matter what other calls you make. You are not going to score a touchdown, kick a field goal, or be able to decline a penalty on the play. The only other option you will have is to go home and fumble the ball (if there is a home left). You're also going to be stuck with your tail between your legs and a lot left for you to think about. The cat or dog can come out to play if it wants to but know that there are consequence to every action and decision you make, so be ready for whatever choice you've made.

When you and your spouse were courting, you took the time to get to know each other. While you were taking that time, you were building up trust, a bond you share between the two of you. While you were building a bond, you knew the person you were building trust with that you'd be able to rely on them no matter what the circumstances. You have arranged for that person to own some part of yourself; you have built a bridge. When that bridge was built, it was built with time and trust; a lot of blood, sweat, and time went into that bridge. You slaved over building that. With that being said, it was built with bricks and mortar, or did you build a bridge with something else?

It's not hard to gain someone's trust (*for the first time*); people give it out so freely these days. Now it does take a little work with some, but for others, it's not so hard. I earned a lot of trust from people due to the angle that I was using. I wanted them to trust me and fall in love with me, and I wanted them to think everything was great between us. Later, I would pull the plug so hard all they would be able to see were stars and they would be dazed. By the time all the smoke cleared, I was gone. I had their heart, feelings, and emotions all in hand, and like salt, I tossed it over my shoulder simply because I had done what I intended to do in the first place. It was easy for me; I had made this my job and priority in life.

Doing all that, in the end, I found that not only did I hurt other people but also it made it hard for me to be in a relationship. It was a fight for me to get through. To be honest, I am still fighting that very fight. I love my king, but sometimes my actions show him differently. He has been strong (to me that's makes him KING by any means) to tolerate all I have done and all that I have said. When you have a strong man, he is supposed to be there for you and to help you get through any and all situations no matter what they are. Living the life I was living was not healthy; the only thing I got out of it was... nothing. I got nothing out of what I was doing, except complete satisfaction at that time. I did waste a lot of my precious time and energy, but all on the wrong people. At the time, I got gratification and that felt good. But after the preliminary impact and mutilation I had done and it was over, I felt I had to do it again because it was only a temporary fix. It was only temporary gratification.

Now if I can do all that to one person and move on, then what do you think that people are going to do when you look over the fence to the other side? What if you are dillydallying around and end up catching feelings for someone whether you have slept with them or not. You can spend a lot of time with a person and catch feelings. Now when they pull the plug on you, what are you going to do? What's your next step? What if she (fellas) ends up pregnant? What if, ladies, you end up pregnant? How are you going to feel? What are you going to do? What is going to happen with all those emotions? What are your thoughts going to be about yourself? How are you going to look at your spouse? How are you going to tell your spouse? If anything, you are going to be twice as grateful for the person you're with (especially if they decide to stick it out with you). What you are going to do is sit back and think, what was I even doing in the first place? What the hell was I thinking? What does the future hold for me now? You're going to have a lot on your mind. You are going to look at your relationship and yourself a lot differently at that point. You now have a situation at hand where you wish you could take back and redo what you've done. You are going to have a lot of questions which need answering. You're also going to have a lot to think about when it comes to your decision-making. Think about this: what if the person you decided to cheat on your spouse/significant other with is a fatal attraction? What if that fatal attraction decides to put your family in harm's way? What is your plan to keep things in order? What are you going to do to keep your family out of harm's way? I bet you didn't think about the consequences beforehand.

Why does/did it take an incident as such to get you to sit down and think? You were being selfish and irrational, and you just had to let yourself give in to temptation. You let your hormones/testosterone do the thinking for you because you were in the heat of the moment. You saw something you wanted, and you went for it. The time was right. You and your spouse were at odds with each other, and it's been a bumpy road for a while. You did what you wanted to do at the time. Whether it was a one-night stand or something which turned into something else, it is going to come back and bite you in the ass. You ever heard of the expression, What you do in the dark will come to light? Well, that's called karma, my friend.

What have you done with the trust you've earned from your spouse? That trust that took so much time to build, you took that and threw it out the door for all your own selfish reasons. Was it worth it? Was it worth the pain and heartache you caused your partner? The only thing you've done is drive a deeper wedge between the both of you. Now your relationship is so far down the well that you have no idea how you are going to swim back up to the top. The well is dry and there is no one on the outside to give you any rope to get out of it. Your significant other is not going to throw you any slack, (s)he would just rather see you struggle and suffer for what you've done.

Are you utilizing all you have put in the marriage or relationship to the best of your ability? Do you have any bridges that need to be repaired? Do you have any idea what needs to be worked on, or have you not paid any attention? Sometimes we leave potholes and welding issues behind when circumstances arise. Sometimes we take a jackhammer to something that didn't need repaired in the first place, so, in turn, we made what wasn't a problem in the beginning a problem to deal with. Have you been looking over the bridge at the grassy knolls on the other side? Have you even seen the maintenance or the upkeep that you have been doing on your side of the fence? Did you break that trust? How are you feeling about the trust that you have between the two of you now?

If your bridge is broken in places or is in the process of being destroyed, then you both need to find out what tools you are going to need in order to repair the damage. As you should already know, this is going to take time, work, and trust from the both of you. Not ONE, but BOTH! It takes two people to work on the relationship, not just one; it doesn't matter who did what. You gave your significant other the option/choice to walk away when you decided to go over and play for the other team. Your actions play a big part in everything you do.

You have to let the past be the past and move forward. I know this is hard to do, but this is what needs to be done. You can forgive each other and move forward with life. There is no need to hold on to what damage has been done. It's not worth the time or the energy. And it's not healthy for you; grudges hold and weigh you down. They're like cylinders tied to your ankles when you're trying to keep your head above water, and you're going to drown. Holding on to damage that was done will be the cause for everything from that point forward to spiral downhill. Reestablishing trust and being 100 percent honest is a hard pill to swallow and a hell of a hill to climb back up, but it's not impossible. Every relationship is worth fighting for, especially when you really want it to work and when you are both in love with each other. Think of it this way, if you don't work it out with your significant other, then you are going to have to go out and start all over again with someone else, and there is a lot of TIME and EFFORT which is going to be involved in that, not only that but you have to get to know them inside and out. I would hate to see someone date someone for a while (let's say six months to a year) and when they crack open the egg, it turns out to be rotten to the core. You have to both want it. You both have to work at it to make it happen. It takes two people to put forth the effort in order for it to be a success.

You both need to understand yourselves as your own individual persons. You can sit down and write on a piece of paper what you struggle with—i.e., communication, flirting, friends, family, in-laws, etc., whatever it is that you are struggling with, even if it's from childhood (something in a conversation can trigger something in or out of you that makes you upset and that's how an argument can start). Maybe your partner is blind to something that you haven't told them, and when a heated argument arises, you shut down. Your partner should be the FIRST person that you talk to about whatever the issue is at hand. You are supposed to be there for each other—comfort, support, and ventilation.

You have to be careful of the seeds you sow. If you don't like what's growing and what is becoming of your relationship then take a look in the mirror and ask yourself, what seed did I plant? There are some plants and fruits that are toxic and toxicity can spread.

WHEN FORCED TO CHOOSE BETWEEN
YOUR CAREER AND YOUR SPOUSE,
YOUR FRIENDS AND YOUR SPOUSE, OR
EVEN YOUR FAMILY AND YOUR SPOUSE,
YOU MUST ALWAYS CHOOSE TO PUT
YOUR SPOUSE AHEAD OF THE REST.
IF YOUR FIRST LOYALTY ISN'T TO YOUR SPOUSE,
THEN YOU DON'T REALLY UNDERSTAND
THE MEANING OF MARRIAGE.

—DAVE WILLIS

Chapter 5

Communication

com·mu·ni·ca·tion
noun \kə-ˌmyü-nə-ˈkā-shən\
: the act or process of using words, sounds, signs,
or behaviors to express or exchange
: information or to express your ideas, thoughts,
feelings, etc., to someone else
: a message that is given to someone: a letter, tele-
phone call, etc.

Yes, communication is such an easy thing to do, right? All you do is sit down, talk, and discuss stuff, and when that's all done, you move on to another topic and talk about that, right? Wrong! Communication and understanding is almost a new language to learn. I, for one, was very bad at communication unless it was something I wanted (that would be me being selfish). With the life in which I was living, I didn't have to communicate too much for the simple fact that I was not in it for the feelings and emotions. I was not trying to let anyone get close to me to get to know who I was as a person. I put up a wall that could not be penetrated.

This seems like the easiest thing in the world to do: talk, text, e-mail, phone calls, video chat. In a world of technology, there are so many ways to communicate. But honestly, do you know what communication is? Most people in the world don't know how to communicate with one another, especially those in marriages or relationships. You learn how to read each other when you are in a relationship (things become/became routine). You do the minimal when you've been with someone for so long. There are things you don't notice, or when you do take notice, it's been going on for so long all you can do is sit down and think about, well, when did this all start? When did we start acting this way? Why don't we talk like we used to? What happened to the conversations we used to have? When did we stop talking to each other? When did we stop bonding?

Sometimes routines can be hard to break; they can also be hard to get into. Some people don't like to make changes when they have a routine, then there are those who are afraid to make changes. Some people get stuck in a routine and don't know how to get out of it. When you are in a relationship, you are supposed to help each other in every way possible no matter what the situation is. You have to lean on each other in every way possible, and you have to be there for each other no matter what the costs are. Don't you remember why you both got together? Don't you remember why you wanted to be with the person you are with?

There is nothing worse than someone who does not want to talk about the situation or problem at hand. No communication at all is not going to solve anything; the problem is not going to go away. Let me use this analogy: Problems can be like your electric bill; if you don't pay a bill the next month, the next bill is going to come in, and it's going to be more than the first one the month before. It is going to be a late fee tagged on, and pretty soon you get a disconnection notice. Unless you call and talk to someone to make arrangements to set up some kind of payment plan, then that utility is going to get cut off and you are going to be in the dark. Problems get more problematic and more expensive the longer you ignore them. It goes from one problem to another problem because the first one didn't get paid any attention to. Everything has a chain reaction: a cause and effect. Whether good or bad there's going to be some kind of outcome.

Why does is seem that the easiest thing to do is the hardest thing to do? It's not at all hard to talk to someone, it's not hard to listen to someone, it's not hard all to sit down with another person and have a conversation. But when it comes to talking about matters with your significant other, which actually means something, that's when all the communication gets tangled in a web. This is the most problematic problem in most relationships. People have a tendency to shut down and stop communicating with their partner, which, as we know, is not going to solve any issues. One person will listen or pretend to listen while the other talks. While the other will talk and think, the other person is listening. The perception we have of other people is usually wrong, which is why it's so important to be on the same page. It can be hard and sometimes unnerving to talk to someone when you are at odds with each other. The only way to solve any situation is to sit down with a clear mind and talk about whatever the problem may be.

Also, keep in mind that not everyone knows how to communicate. Some people don't know how to talk to each other without getting frustrated, some people don't know how to say what they want to say, some people don't know how to start to communicate, some people don't know if what they're say is going to come across in an off tone or taken the wrong way. If you must, get a piece of paper and write all your thoughts down as to what you want to talk about, what's on your mind, and what's bothering you. This can make things a little easier. Don't think you can remember what it is you want to say because you can forget and your mind can play tricks on you. What you can do is give that paper to your significant other and let him/her read what you wrote. Some people have a hard time expressing themselves due to them not wanting to come across in a way that's going to be negative. If you need to, sit down and write a letter and try to explain yourself that way.

"Being able to say what's on your mind helps to relieve stress and buildup of un necessary thoughts and helps to express yourself. The truth can and will hurt when you ask someone for honesty. So be careful what you ask for; if you can't handle the delivery, don't place the order" (Cheekz).

Each person has a different way of communicating. You may talk to each other about everyday activities (the kids, work, their day, parents, etc.), but that is repetitious and everyday communication and it's not really considered communication. You may be talking, but it's not about nothing of major concern, if you will. You say enough to each other to get you both through the day. It's about everyday life and the habits you have. When it comes to the problems, you have a different way of communicating with each other. I know, I know, I know, it can be hard to just sit and put your differences aside for a moment and listen to your partner and where they are coming from. All the huffing and puffing and all the sighing show signs of disinterest and should not be done because the last thing you are going to do is listen. Don't worry, you both can hear each other out and listen to where each one of you are coming from and come up to a solution. Yes, I know everything is much easier said than done. But practice makes perfect.

Do you actually understand what it is your spouse/significant other is saying to you? Do you really understand what they are going through? Do you understand what the problem is? Do you understand what it is they are going through? Do you see them trying to reach out to you? Are you trying to reach out and communicate with your significant other? Are you talking to someone else about the problems you are having in your marriage or relationship? If you are talking to someone else about the problems you are having in your marriage or relationship, it should be someone who is a licensed counselor or even another couple who have experienced what you both are going through. You can't go to someone who has no knowledge of your experience or someone that is single because they are not going to understand. The first thing they might tell you is "See, that's why I'm not in a relationship because of that reason."

When you communicate, you have to learn how to regurgitate what each other is saying, example, "I don't like the fact that you hang out with the boys more than you hang out with me." In return, you can say, "So what I am understanding from what you said is, you think I am spending too much time with the guys?"

Everything you say can be interpreted in a different way to someone else. Just because you think one way does not mean the other person thinks the same way. You have to make sure you both have a clear understanding of the subject at hand. There is no need to get an attitude, get frustrated, or get mad. Take time with each other to see what each other wants and needs are. You both have to take a time out to understand each other in order for anything to work. You also need to make sure you articulate your words so you both will grasp the concept of what the other is saying or trying to say.

Communication is almost a dying language because everyone wants to text/e-mail each other, and that's not a way of talking or hashing things out. I can never say this enough: the power of the tongue is extremely dangerous. It can tear someone apart in a matter of seconds. Be very careful with the words you choose to use; you should always think before you speak. And always pay attention to how you say what you say. I know that's easier said than done, but practice makes perfect. You should always be building each other up, never tearing each other down. (Now there are times where someone needs to be torn down, but in the same instance, you should build them right back up.) It makes no difference if you're having an argument or not, NEVER tear each other down and not rebuild. Always remember you are both ONE UNIT.

* * *

Death and life are in the power of the tongue:
and they that love it shall eat the fruit thereof.
—Proverbs 18:21

After getting married, the woman is supposed to be submissive to her significant other. It only takes a moment to listen and understand what the other is trying to say. The man is the head of the household, whether he is the breadwinner or not. The woman, after getting married, has to be submissive to her significant other. You also have to know when to step up when the king makes a mistake or something has happened to where he needs his queen to take control. Let me break things down here for a bit. First, let's explain what a hierarchy is.

Hierarchy: a ruling body of clergy organized into orders or ranks, each subordinate to the one above it, especially the bishops of a province or nation

King (noun): a male monarch of a major territorial unit, especially one whose position is hereditary & who rules for life

Queen (noun): a female monarch

Partner: spouse, companion, significant other

Husband (noun): a male partner in a marriage

Wife (noun): a female partner in a marriage

I'm not here to give you a vocabulary lesson by any means, but sometimes, we, as individuals, tend to forget what the meaning of words are and how they can be used to empower or hurt someone else. I wrote this so you can have an understanding of the meaning of the words because, sometimes, we all forget we have a place. We also can forget what the meaning of the words or titles stand for. You both have a responsibility in the marriage or relationship, whether you want to believe it or not. When you both work at doing your job in the marriage or relationship, everything is balanced. When one falls short, the other's job is to be there to help and let the other know that they are either slacking on their job or forgetting. When the both of you have differences and at each other's throat, you have no order and things are in disarray. Time for you both to sit down to communicate and solve the problem to get the house back in order; without order, there can and will be other disruptions, and those disruptions will allow for the inevitable to happen. What you allow to happen is by choice, not by chance.

In all things, there is a chain of command that must be followed. As the man being the head of household, he must be as such, feel as such, and do as such. Women, we have to let the man know he is in fact the king of the house. He is the deciding factor (but not without hearing the queen). Men can't just make all the decisions about what is going or not going to happen, what is or not going to be done around the house, etc. When there is a problem at hand, then he needs to sit down with you and talk about a solution and options. Men, you also have to communicate with your queen as to the things that are going on financially, emotionally, spiritually, or anything in general. No matter what the situation is, COMMUNICATION and UNDERSTANDING between the both of you is what's going to get you both and your family through whatever it is you're going through. I am not saying that the man makes all the decisions, he does have to speak with his spouse or significant other before he makes any decision. The man may be the head of the house but we know the "woman" runs the home!

Not all of us like to talk in the heat of the moment, and not all of us like to tackle the situations which arise in our relationship. Not all of us are able to handle communicating about any problem at all. The fact remains it's a matter of life, and nothing can change what happens in life. If you have a hard time trying to talk to your significant other, you can always write things down on a notepad and deliver the message to him/her verbally from there. Any form of communication is better than no form of communication at all. If you do communicate but you don't do it much, you can find subjects to talk about that entertain you or amuse you. For example, I like to watch Animal Planet; they have documentaries about animals. Let's take for instance lions. I like to watch how the lionesses work as a team to hunt for food and bring it back to the family to eat, but before anyone can eat, the lion himself, the king of the jungle, eats first. When speaking with my significant other, I can say, "I like how they work as a team, and I think that's something we should do or try." I would like to take a moment right here to say that no matter what, throughout the day, you should tell your significant other that you love them, randomly as the days go by. It doesn't matter if it's by text, flowers, phone call, a candy, a note, telegraph, e-mail, Glide, Tango, Skype, or whatever form of communication you have. Saying these words and meaning what you say go a long way for someone. You never know what kind of day your significant other is having, and just the sight of you saying something so endearing can be great gratification to them in that moment.

Let's Take a Break

INTERMISSION 2

They're both getting dressed to go out for a night on the town; they are both long overdue for a night out. It's been a rough week for them with all that's going on. Renovations being done to the house. Working sixty-five hours a week, trying to get deadlines met. They know they both need to unwind and have some time to enjoy life. She's in the room, putting on a sexy red body-fitting dress with a pair of thigh-highs and gold shoes which match her gold clutch. He is going to wear black pants, white shirt, gold vest, black blazer, gold cuff links, and a gold handkerchief. He walks ever so smoothly over to his wife and stands behind her while she sits in her chair, looking in her vanity. He says to her, "I will see you when you get there." She smiles a crafty smile as he bends down to kiss her on the cheek and walks out the room. She puts on the final touches of her makeup and sprays on the sexiest of fragrance; she applies it behind her ears, on her neck, and on both her wrists. She gets up, grabs her clutch, and walks out of the room.

She makes her way downstairs; as she reaches the bottom of the steps, she looks herself over in the mirror one good long time and prances around to see how seductively she can look—checking every inch of her body and how the dress hugs on her, pushing her breast up, hugging her curves, and gripping her ass, looking like a sexy piece of candy waiting to be eaten. She smiles and stops, admiring herself, and rechecks her makeup to make sure she looks flawless. She walks toward the kitchen, grabs her keys, and heads for the garage.

She drives along the road, listening to "Real Quick Loving" by J. Thompson, a nice sexy jazz tune which relaxes her and places her in another realm. That song alone makes her think of her husband and the sex they have. How he made a pathway of candles from the door to the bedroom. All along the steps, leaving notes with a chocolate-covered strawberry on a dish along the pathway. When she reached the bedroom, there was a bottle of champagne, him lying on the bed naked with rose petals all over his naked body. The thought of that sent a rush through her body, causing her to secrete, making her want to turn the car around and call her husband. She snaps out of it, and before she knows it, she's pulling up to her destination and valet parking. She waits for the valet attendant to open the door and help her out the car; she steps out looking absolutely ravishing. The doorman escorts her to the front entrance and opens the door. She walks in and informs the hostess she would like to sit at the bar. She makes her way over to the bar, feeling the eyes of all the men in the room staring at her as she walks in with her five-inch heels and her form-fitting red dress with gold clutch under her forearm.

She makes her way to the bar and sits down, crosses her long silky legs, and gets the attention of the bartender. She places an order for a martini (watermelon) and places her clutch on the counter. She then feels the presence of a man behind her, but she does not let him know she notices him. He says to her, "Let me get that drink for you, beautiful." She allows him to pay for her drink. "Why are you here in this place all alone?" he asks. She replies, "I needed to get away from all the chaos of the world, so this is where I came to unwind." He says, "Well, naturally, I can understand that. Do you mind if I sit next to you?" She looks at the empty seat as if to say it's yours if you want it. He sits down and engages in conversation with her; she looks as though she is interested in what he is saying, but she isn't really listening.

The man sitting in the back can see all that is going on from the corner of the room and just admires all the men checking out this woman. He is in the back of the lounge in a chair where there is very little lighting; he's smoking on a cigar, looking at all the people in the room, and notice they're all gawking at this lovely walking statue, which was strutting in the door. He takes notice as well, looking at her long gorgeous legs and her sexy walk. He hears one man say, "Wow, she is absolutely gorgeous, and I would love to be the one she comes home to every night." As he sits and hears all the murmurs of other men talking, an old colleague of his takes notice to him sitting alone in the corner. They haven't seen each other since college, so they sit and talk about the old days and catch each other up on what's been going on in their lives. They talk about basketball and how one was better than the other in college, and his colleague also talks about all the women they used to have while in college; they laughed and exchanged numbers, and he departed, leaving his friend alone at the table.

A few minutes later, the bartender comes back over with her drink and places it in front of her, and he lets the bartender know that he needs a refill. He pays for both of the drinks and tips the bartender while she hurries off to fix him another drink; he stares at the lovely lady beside him. As he stares, he basks in the essence of her smell. As they were in conversation, another man approaches her from the right side and he grabs a seat next to her. He orders a scotch on the rocks, his voice deep, low, and sexy. As he ordered his drink, the sound of his voice sent chills up and down her spine and made its way down to her clitoris and made her wet. The bass of his voice did something to her. She closed her eyes took a drink and imagined his hands feeling on her breast, caressing her skin and feeling all over her body. The sound of his baritone voice in her ear, whispering to her what she wants to hear. The man that was talking to her decided he was going to leave her with his name and number on a napkin and left to talk business with a colleague of his.

As he left, she turned to her right and saw the man which was sitting beside her at the bar. He was dark with the most beautiful of skin dressed to kill. He smelled like he wanted to be eaten alive. He says to her, "How is your night going, beautiful lady?" She turns to him and says, "So far, my night is going quite well, as a matter of fact." As she picks up her drink and takes a sip of her martini, she asks, "And how has your night been, Mr....?" He says, "I apologize, beautiful. My name is Thomas, Eric Thomas." As he introduces himself, he takes her hand and kisses her hand, smelling all her essence. She replies, "My name is Kelly, and it's nice to make your acquaintance, Mr. Thomas." He replies, "Much obliged. Would you please, Ms. Kelly, accompany me to an evening dinner if you're not expecting anyone? As lovely as you are, I would be the least bit surprised if you are expecting someone." She looks at him for a few moments and says, "Sure, why not?" To his astonishment, he takes her hand and guides her to the booth in which they will be sitting.

They walk over to the table which he's already reserved, and he lets her slide in the booth first, and he follows after. She asks, "What is it that you do for a living, Mr. Thomas?" Eric tells her that he's an engineer for a company right outside of town. They go on with the chitter-chatter, getting to know each other until the waitress shows up. She asks if they are ready to order, and without notice, neither one has looked at the menu as they have been engaged in each other's conversation for the past fifteen minutes. They politely ask her to come back in a few minutes to give them time to look at the menu. As they laugh, they look over the menu and are now ready to order; the waitress comes back in just enough time to break the silence and the gazing they have on each other.

He placed an order for the both of them: they had the duet duck and Dungeness, which consisted of parfait of Oregon black truffle, roasted Puyallup duck foie gras, foie gras sabayon sandwich of Dungeness crab with apple foie gras ferine, coriander, and a bottle of 1962 Domaine De La Romanee-Conti-Romanee Grad Cru, Cote de Nuits, France.

After placing their order, the waitress kindly removes their menus and asks if they need refills on their drinks. He orders another scotch, and he turns to ask if she would like another drink. She replies, "No, I am fine for now. Thank you." The waitress disappears, and they are once again left alone with each other. They stare intently in each other's eyes. He coddles her face, bringing her in closer to him, and they kiss ever so softly but with so much intention, not noticing that the other men in the room have watched the two of them together. They talk among themselves at how they would love to be in his shoes right now and how the night would end for her if they were in his position. One guy chimes in to say, "Well, I bought her her first drink until Rich came over cock blockin', wanting to talk business deals." They all laugh and say, "And you didn't see that old trick coming. That's one of the oldest tricks in the book. I got you away from her, and now neither one of us are in the company of her presence."

As they are laughing and joking with one another, Kelly and Eric gaze at each other and get lost in each other's eyes. Not paying any attention to who is watching them, they start kissing each other passionately, like they want to eat each other. Her hand caresses his face as their lips touch. His hand finds their way on her warm thighs, crawling up toward her womanhood. They both stop noticing that they were getting hot and heavy pretty fast.

The onlookers were staring, and some were even jealous of the two who seemed to have hit it off well from the start. She asked to be excused from the table, and he got up to let her out and he followed. They went to the women's restroom with heavy panting and kissing and made it to the stall with all the heavy panting, and he raised her dress and pulled down her panties. She took off his belt and unbuttoned and unzipped his pants. He let them fall to the floor, and she readies for him and pulls his manhood out of his pants and places it inside of her. He had sex with her like a ravaging machine, making her moan while scratching at his clothes. They have sex in the stall, not caring if someone enters or not. "Yes, baby, yes, you're in the right spot… Damn, you making me feel so good…Give it to me harder," she whispers in his ear as she sucks. He says to her, "Damn, baby, this feels so good to me, wrapping around me like a wet sponge. Nobody can make you feel better than I can. Nobody can serve you as well as I can." She responds back to him, "And you are the only one that can get it, baby. You know how to make this pussy cry. You know how to make it wet."

They're both about to climax, both getting sweaty and sticky. As she gets ready to orgasm, she screams out, "I'm about to…I'm about to come." And he says he is too. They both come, and he lets her down and places his fingers inside of her womanhood and tastes the nectar of her orgasm and says, "Now let's go eat." He walks out of the stall and heads to the men's restroom to clean himself up, and she cleans herself up in the ladies' room. She walks out, and he is there to greet her at the table. He lets her sit down and goes in behind her. As they are getting readjusted, their food is on its way to the table. They sit and laugh, and she says, "Honey, that was, by far, the best experience we have had in a long time." He says to her, "Yes, it was and we are going to have to do something like that again and make it more enticing." They laugh and giggle and start eating dinner. This was the night they both need, and it had the best ending to a week of chaos in a long time.

A MAN THAT TRULY LOVES A WOMAN

❖   IS MORE CONCERNED WITH SPENDING
TIME THAN SPENDING MONEY.

❖   IS HER LEADER, NOT DICTATOR.

❖   DOES NOT CHEAT BECAUSE HE
KNOWS HE'D BE CHEATING HIMSELF.

❖   GIVES HER FREEDOM, NOT CAPTIVITY.

❖   ENCOURAGES HER DREAMS
WHILE CHASING HIS.

❖   SHOWS HER OFF TO THE WORLD
BECAUSE HER LIGHT IN HIS LIFE

❖   IS SO BRIGHT HE CAN'T HIDE IT.

I THINK A LOT OF US HAVE A MISUNDERSTANDING
ABOUT WHAT A REAL MAN'S LOVE LOOKS LIKE.

—TONY A. GASKINS JR.

Chapter 6

Work

work
noun \wərk\
: a **job or activity that you do regularly** especially in order to earn money
: **the place where you do your job**
: the things that you do **especially as part of your job**

1a: sustained physical or mental effort to **overcome obstacles and achieve** an objective or **result**
b: the labor, task, or duty that is one's accustomed means of **livelihood**
9a: effective operation: EFFECT, RESULT [*wait for time to do its healing work*]

All this and now we come to the work. I bet you thought you did a lot of work up until this point, but there's more. Now I know all of us don't like to clock in for work on a daily basis, and at times, we get up in the morning drudging to go to work. We even think about calling off because we don't really feel like going in. Most of us know if we don't work, we are going to lose out on money to get the bills paid, so we go in anyway. When this occurs, we have a different attitude about work and we just do enough to get through the day. We put on that work face, i.e., work smile and work attitude, just to get by. Some people at work you can fool and others you can't.

By all means, don't let your relationship reflect any part of the work attitude.

We've been through a lot already, haven't we? It seems as though we have. I bet you never thought of all the work you put into a relationship until you both got into an argument and one of you wanted to call it quits. The minute someone says that it's over, bells get to ring in your head, and you sit down and think about all the time, money, and energy spent into the relationship; you start to have second thoughts. Wait a minute, what do you mean you want to call it quits and we've been together for five-plus years? It's not about to end that easy. This is where more work comes in simply because you have to fix all that is wrong. I don't know if you know this or not, but this is going to be more work than usual. Fixing things that are wrong in a relationship require a lot more work. If you would have taken the time to fix the situation before it got this far, you would not have had to put in so much overtime. You reap what you sow.

All that was a lot of work, and there is always more work to do, especially when you are trying to fix the problem(s) at hand. Fixing any issue or problem is going to take work, time, and communication from the both of you. This is where you are not going to be able to half step any of the process.

We all know and learned that you have to crawl before you walk, and this is true in all and everything you do no matter what it is. You can't just do something and take off running and think you are going to be good at it, let alone a success. If this was the case, we would all be rich and doing what we all want to do, have what we want and not want for anything. There would be no desire to stride for anything else in life; you would then, in return, become bored with nothing else to strive or work toward. You have to apply the same logic to your relationship. First you crawl, then you take baby steps, then you learn how to balance yourself and learn to walk, and soon you learn how to run so on and so forth.

When it comes to relationships, sometimes you have to go back to the basics and start over from scratch. There is nothing wrong with that, but you shouldn't have to get to that point. You need to get out of the way you are thinking and start thinking on a different level, start thinking outside the box. What I mean by that is, you have to allow your mind to open up and look at things from a different perspective, and I know that is not always an easy thing to do; this is going to take some work. You literally have to start all over again and go back down memory lane. Look at the things you can change, look at what you can make better, and look at different options.

You both are going to have to make sacrifices for each other when it comes to putting work into the relationship. You might have to rearrange your schedules in order to make time for each other to get down to the situation at hand. You may have to let something go in order to put things back in order. You also might have to let some friends go that are getting in the way of the time you are going to need in order to spend with your significant other. You are both going to have to come to some kind of agreement and arrangement in order to put in the necessary work to get things done.

There is nothing wrong with going back to the basics to make it work. There is nothing wrong with telling your significant other how you feel and what you feel. There is nothing wrong with giving output on what and where you think the relationship is going. You have to make sure you both are always up-front and honest with each other even if that means the truth is going to hurt. You can respect each other more when the truth is told. You can work at things when the truth is out in the open.

When you tell a little white lie, it can and will come back to bite you in the butt. You have to work so much harder at covering up a lie rather than telling the honest truth. When you tell the truth, you have options, and when you tell a lie, you create more work for you and your significant other to deal with. We don't need the scenario that was introduced in the beginning of the book; no one wants to go through that. You know the consequences behind lying: you have to rebuild trust, respect, and loyalty and you have to put in overtime to get the situation right again. You lose so much when you lie. Is your significant other worth lying to? Is your relationship worth the sacrifice of a lie? Once you lie and then, in turn, you turn around and tell the truth, who is going to believe you? That's like crying wolf all the time; the one time you do tell the truth, no one is going to believe you.

Everything you do has consequences and repercussions, which was all learned as a child. There can be a domino effect for the actions of your lie, so save yourself the aggravation, time, and humility in the beginning.

You also have to take a step back and analyze the situation at hand before you can start working on it. Work is never an easy thing to do, especially when you have to work five (or more) days a week. It becomes draining and very tiring, and relationships are no different. No one likes to be humiliated; no one likes being made a fool of.

Relationships are hard; no one said it would be easy. You have to put in a lot of energy to make it right when there has been so many wrongdoings. You have to put in overtime when so much has gone wrong. Time, work, trust, loyalty, and communication are all factors in the recovery process. Things go by so much easier and smoother when you can communicate your feelings and problems and situations to each other. Yes, this is going to be work but not half as much when one has betrayed the other or you both have betrayed each other.

It can be easy to forgive each other, but it's hard for someone to forget the wrongdoings. Don't EVER throw up in each other's face what the other one has done wrong. Once you've decided to forgive someone for what they have done to you, then let it be, leave it alone, and move on. Bringing up things from the past is only going to cause complications and arguments. We know that arguments are going to lead you back to square one with each other. Let's move on from square one to square two and get the recovery process on the move.

Work at being positive for each other. Work at spending more time with each other. Work at learning how to forgive. Work at leaving what's in the past. Work at telling each other how you feel. Work at loving each other. Work at being there for each other. Work at being a unit. Work at being a support system for each other. Work at being a stronger unit. Work on yourself as an individual even if that means that you have to go to counseling. Work on all the problems you have—make a list, sit down, and talk. Work, work, work.

NOTHING IS GOING TO BE EASY, AND NOTHING IS GOING TO FALL OUT OF THE SKY TO HELP YOU. YOU HAVE TO HELP YOURSELF AND EACH OTHER. DON'T BE A PUNK OR STOP BEING A PUNK AND GET IT TOGETHER TO SAVE WHAT YOU HAVE. Build or re-build one another up. If you're being negative or a crutch then you don't want it, any part of it. Stop being a pussy and either man-up or woman-up because it takes two people to build a solid foundation in the marriage or relationship.

Chapter 7

Loyalty

loy·al·ty
noun\ˈlȯi(-ə)l-tē\
: the quality or state of being loyal
: a loyal feeling: a feeling of strong support for someone or something

How hard is it really to be loyal to someone? It's not hard at all especially if it's being loyal to someone that you love. It should be something that comes honestly, naturally, and without grief. I can say that it has never been hard for me to be loyal to someone that I'm with. Being there for someone when they need it most is the best thing that you can do for your relationship even if that means one of you are not cooperating in the best of manners. Regardless of how you feel, you need to be there for each other through all the ups and downs of life. It is a bumpy roller-coaster ride when you are in a marriage or relationship, but if it was built on the building block foundation listed in chapter 2, then you are not going to have that hard of a time getting through any issue, but it will be hard.

I hate to say this, but LOYALTY is a big word for a lot of us, and it shouldn't be, especially for those that have been married or together for a while. After you've found the one you want and desire to be with for the rest of your life, this word becomes like a glove to your hand. Loyalty is what you worked so hard to build up in your relationship. There is nothing better than trust and loyalty when you are with the person that you love. It keeps a grudge off your shoulders. Neither one of you should have a problem with being able to forgive. When you know you are being loyal to your significant other, there is no better feeling in the world. You have no worries, and nothing is going to come out of the closet later down the road to hurt you.

Loyalty to each other is like being in a contract with a cell phone company. You can go to another company if you want to, but things are not going to be the same. In a relationship, things can't always be the same, but there still needs to be some consistency on both your ends. First of all, you know that if your contract is not up, you are going to have to pay an early termination fee and pay the last phone bill (and we all know cell phone companies charge you for service a month in advance). That would be significant to getting a divorce; you are going to pay out of your own pocket and you all know how expensive that is. When you switch to another company, you are going to have money for another phone, and the service is going to be different, meaning, you might not receive all your calls, your phone may not work in certain areas of the house like the old one did, it may not have the same apps you had on your other phone, it may not work as fast, or it may have a different call quality. In layman's terms, you may not want the same thing all the time; you just want and need to make some improvements or changes to what you have already so it can fit both your needs. It's a lot easier to stick it out with the old company than to switch because you never know what you are getting. In essence, it is easier to stick it out with the one that you are with, due to the fact it's easier to iron out problems you're having as opposed to finding new problems to deal with. No one wants to read all the fine print or try to read between the lines to try to figure out what it is they are getting. All that adds up to a headache and a painful mess, which no one wants to deal with.

Why is it so hard to be loyal for some? There could be a number of reasons:

1. Falling out of love
2. Not feeling the same
3. Losing interest
4. Grass looking greener on the other side
5. Mad at too many disagreements or arguments
6. Frustration
7. Feeling insecure

There are a multitude of reasons why people will feel like they don't want to be loyal to someone. What do you do when you start feeling this way? Well, for one, you need to talk to your partner. You have to remember that you both were each other's best friend in the beginning of the relationship, when you were getting to know each other. You have to get back to talking to each other, being inquisitive, asking questions (don't make assumptions, always ask questions). Get to the bottom of whatever the issue is, and tell the truth even if the truth hurts. In life, it is better knowing the truth as opposed to a little white lie, being when that little white lie comes out of the closet, then you are going to have to explain why you lied in the first place. This is just going to make things so much harder on the both of you. There is nothing better than hearing the honest truth from your spouse/significant other or, as I like to put it, hearing it straight from the horse's mouth.

When you are with someone that you love and care about, you have to give them your all, and I mean all of you—all your time and consideration. You have to be completely dedicated to each other, be there for each other in good times and bad times, not just when you feel the need to be. Marriage or relationships are not easy, and no one said it was going to be easy. You learn from all you do and all that you go through in your marriage or relationship. Yes, we all make mistakes, and some are a lot worse than others, but if your marriage is worth saving, then those mistakes are mediocre and not worth killing the marriage or relationship over.

It's not hard to be loyal to the one you love the most. It is hard to rebuild all that you worked so hard to build in the first place, but it can be done with both of you putting the effort forward. You both have so much to look forward to in life, so work at making your home a better home. There are times in which you have to sit back and look at things from each other's perspective. Like I said before, marriage or relationships are a two-way street. Everyone has their viewpoints on things, and you have to take into consideration what those are.

Chapter 8

Love

love
noun\ˈləv\
: a feeling of strong or constant affection for a person
: attraction that includes sexual desire: the strong affection felt by people who have a romantic relationship
: a person you love in a romantic way

Do you remember the first time you fell in love? Do you remember the feeling of loving and being loved in return? Remember the smile it put on your face and how it made your heart skip a beat when you saw him/her or talked to him/her on the phone? It made you feel all giddy inside and made you the happiest person on earth. It even made some other folks jealous because of who you were with. It was like a dream come true. You never knew you could feel that way. You didn't think that there was someone out there that could make you feel that good. You loved that particular person because of how they made you feel about yourself, and you liked being seen with them. You loved being together all the time, every minute of every day; there was no one else out there for you. It doesn't matter at what time in your life you felt love from another person, or the thought of feeling love from another person. In that moment, you were happy, and there was no better feeling in the world. It's time to get right back to that very feeling.

There is no stronger word on earth than the word *love*. To tell someone that you love them and mean it is the best feeling in the world to your significant other. There is no better game changer like telling someone you love them, whether you mean it or not. LOVE is a very powerful and valuable four-lettered word, so is HATE. It should not be used loosely. When you tell someone you love them, make sure you tell them the truth and tell them how and why you love them. Example, "Yes, we are close and I feel we have a good friendship and I love our friendship. I like the fact that we have been friends for as long as we have and we have the best friendship, but I am falling in love with you."

"I acknowledge the fact that we are friends and we have been for a good amount of time. But truth of the matter is, I have some kind of feelings for you. I don't know if I am in love with you, but I do know I have something for you. I am not looking to complicate things, so I am going to have to take a step back and analyze the situation."

Now with all that being said, you put the ball in the other person's court. They might feel the same way you do, but you won't know anything until one of you speaks up.

People throw the *love* word around like it's water. One minute someone loves you and the very next minute they don't want nothing to do with you because of something you did or because of the outcome of a situation. Love is something that is 100 percent real, and no matter what kind of love it is, love is love.

There is nothing more beautiful than being in love with the one you are with. Nothing feels so good. Nothing else can put those butterflies in your stomach or put that spark in your eye and make you feel all giddy inside. Love is a beautiful thing when you come across the right person to share it with. Love is not easy to find, especially when you're looking for it. But when you do find it, it's the most lasting memorable thing in life. You can't forget how that feels and you can't forget how the both of you fell for each other.

"All relationships are based on different foundations; the ones that last a lifetime are the ones that are built on trust & honesty, the kind that merits conversations that are both open and true" (Unknown).

If you don't let yourself love again, then you are not going to do anything but hurt yourself in the end. In order to love again, you have to learn how to forgive. You are not going to have anyone to blame but you, all because you did not want to take that chance again. You have to remember what it felt like the first time it happened. You can't let the memory of the person that hurt you stand in the way of your happiness. Yes, I said just that, considering that at the beginning of this book, I was telling you about my story and how I had to get my revenge and how I did men because I was hurt so bad. Yes, I did do what I did, but now that I look back on it and how life has made me change, I am so glad that I am able to love again. Nothing has put a twinkle in my eye and butterflies in my stomach like being in love. I don't regret what I did and what I've went through; it all taught me something. I was able to write this book. I was able to evaluate myself as a person. I was able to go back and look at all the mistakes and wrong turns I made in life. I was able to look at some of the messed-up decision I've made. But I also gained a lot of experiences, came across some very amazing people. I was able to diversify myself into who I am today.

Now if you ask me would I do it all over again, then my answer would be no. I have been on a self-discovery mission most of my life, and in the process, I look back, and I know I could've made better choices and other sacrifices that would've given me a different outcome.

But all in all, I am not mad about the person I am today. I am proud of who I am. None of us are proud about all the things we have done in the past but everything that we have been through and have done has taught us something in life and made us better and stronger in some ways. We go through things to share our experiences with someone else that may be going through something similar.

I don't mind sharing my feelings and letting someone know what I think or how something made me feel. I don't mind being the one someone wants to vent to when they are mad and need to let off some steam. I don't mind being that shoulder someone can cry on. But believe me, I need the same thing at times when I go through things, and that is what your significant other is for.

I remember the first time I fell in love. I loved that man with all my heart and all my being. But now, now it is so different and so much more powerful than the first time. That leap to love, for me, was so hard in the beginning I didn't know what to do. I'm glad I took that step because I don't know where I would be in life had I not done just that. I don't know exactly when it happened, but what I do know is, I have no regrets. I have never in my life loved someone so much and so hard, not the way I do now. When I think about how much I love him, I smile and then I cry. I am not a person of emotions (not showing emotions/feelings) for everyone else to see. I love harder now than I ever did before, maybe that one time being once but that once is enough. I know the difference, and I can feel the difference.

When you love someone, you have to give them your all, and I do mean your ALL. You have to let them know that they're the apple of your eye; you have to let them know that they're number one in your life and they come before everyone else no matter what. Love is not something you can put aside and try to figure out if you want to do something with it or not. You can't play with someone else's time and feelings because feelings are not to be played with, nor is it something that you can just take advantage of. Love is very fragile, and although it is an emotion, it's a very delicate emotion.

There are so many subtle ways to show the one you love that you care for them deeply. You can do it in the privacy of your own home. You can send flowers or an edible arrangement to their job. You can pack their lunch and put a note or card in there to let you know you are thinking about them. You can take them out to lunch or dinner. You can plan an evening out together or with the kids. You can do something as simple as be at home together alone and watch a movie snuggled up on the couch, it could lead to some fun! Never get tired of telling your significant other that you love them and how much you care about them. Relationships require work and time; it took you time to get to where you are, and it's going to take work, time, and dedication from the both of you to keep it all together. It does not matter what you go through; as long as you let the other person know what your true feelings are, you will have done your part.

Consider yourself lucky to have found someone to fall in love with. Not everyone can find love, not everyone has someone to come home to at night. There are people out here looking for love, and there are people out here wanting what you have with your significant other. Finding someone you are compatible with is not an easy task. Be grateful for who you have in your life, and you should spend each day letting each other know how grateful you are. You may not be able to right your wrongs, but you are able to get past any situation.

Finding your equal, your "soul mate," is a very exhausting task for some. Some are out here still looking for what you've already found in each other. Don't be selfish, step-up to the plate and do your part to make it work.

Sex

Yes, yes, yes, the moment I have been waiting for. Well, we have been waiting for. We have finally gotten to the subject I love to talk about. I don't think you need a definition for this one at all! Sex, sex, sex, sex, sex or making love, whatever you want to call it, is the best part of all the fun. Now don't get me wrong; sex is fun, but it also goes above and beyond the fun in the bedroom. It has beneficial factors to your life in general you may or may not know about, which will be explained throughout this chapter.

Am I promoting sex? Why, yes, of course, I am. Like I said before, I don't think there is anything better than great sex, food, and good conversation. I think that is what we all use to enjoy life. You may and might think otherwise, and by all means, that's your right.

Now, ladies, you do have to remember you cannot deny your husband/significant other your sweet nectar. There are so many reasons to have sex. Sex is very beneficial to both your bodies and is actually is good for you.

Benefits of sex:

- You will get sick a lot less.
- It boosts your libido.
- It lowers your blood pressure (the diastolic blood pressure).
- It improves your bladder control.

- It's exercise (I believe we all know that). It improves cardio-vascular fitness, strength, flexibility, and balance (I believe all the men will enjoy his woman being flexible) and emotional health.
- It lowers your risk of heart attack.
- It blocks pain.
- For men, it can make prostate cancer less likely.
  - Frequent ejaculation, especially in twenty-year-old men, may reduce the risk of prostate cancer later in life.
  - Men who had five or more ejaculation weekly while in their twenties reduce their risk of getting prostate cancer later by one-third.
- It improves your sleep.
- It is stress reducer.
- It can reduce the risk of a heart attack if sex is performed more than twice a week.
- It strengthens your well-being.
- Having orgasms increase levels of oxytocin called the love hormone.
  - This hormone helps us to bond and build trust.
  - It helps us gives us the urge to nurture and bond.
  - It helps endorse sleep.
  - It reduces pain, headaches, arthritic pain, and PMS.

On a more personal level, ladies, doing a few pelvic exercises (Kegel exercise) during sex or throughout the day offers benefits to you in the long run.

- You enjoy more pleasure.
- It strengthens the area.
- It helps minimize the risk of incontinence later in life (which is the inability or failure to restrain your sexual appetite)
- It can make sex more enjoyable.

- It can help to avert prolapse (a slipping out position) of the vagina, uterus, and bladder.

Ladies, you can always go out and purchase some Kegel balls or order them online. You don't have to do it for his benefit. Do it for your own benefit. It helps to keep you nice and firm.

So you both need to cut out all the attitude and get busy; it will make you feel better.

Now granted that many of us don't think about the benefits of having sex. We are in it for the feeling we get out of it and the person we are with—how they make us feel, how they touch us, and that orgasm, oh, yes, that orgasm. We may be in it for the wrong reasons, but no matter the reason we are doing it, what we are doing is good for us. Not just for the women but for the men as well. It's good to keep a healthy appetite.

At this point, you both should not be able to get enough of each other; you have come to a point where you have shared your thoughts and considerations when it comes to sex. It should be like it was when you first met, unless it was not the best experience. You both know what you want from each other, and you both know how the other wants to feel. You both know that things can get spicy, and sex can change for the better. You've gotten enough courage to tell the other what is expected of the other, so things should be going smoothly at this point.

You have learned how to feel yourself, understand yourself, and know what it is you like. You have learned how to let go and tap into that inner goddess you have. That inner goddess does not need to be tamed; she needed to be let loose and free so she can be herself. You have learned to become that real freak in the bedroom. You've learn to let go, stop being shy, and bashful. You have learned to understand what it is your king wants from you. Men, you also have to let your woman show you what it is that she wants from you, and you have to be the one to deliver.

By now you should have learned more about yourself; you should know what it is that you like or love about you. You should know how you like to be touched, handled, and played with. You should know more about yourself than you did at the beginning of this book. You should give yourself a round of applause. You came out of that shell, and you let your inner goddess take over and let her be at peace with who she is. She should be strutting around knowing that she has what it is that her man needs and wants. She should be on cloud nine.

That inner goddess has to come out every now and then to get what it is that she craves—satisfaction. Don't keep her locked up and away for too long; let her come out and enjoy what it is that she wants to indulge in. You need to strut around the house looking like you need the attention of your king. Men, you should give her all the attention she needs and help feed that ego she has. You should be able to walk around in a pair of heels and a tutu if you want to. You should be able to let your hair down and be who the goddess wants to be when she is ready to hang out.

I have dealt with a lot of issues in my life; I have overcome a lot of obstacles. I am nowhere near perfect and still have some work to do, but everything gets better with time and age.

What part of your marriage or relationship are you willing to work on? Are you willing to save your marriage or relationship? Are you willing to make things right and better? You should work on all parts of your marriage or relationship together; it takes two to make it work. Remember that you can't get the time back that you have missed or messed up. You can't dissolve anything by not doing anything. You have to set your pride or ego aside and know that the man/woman you are with is worth fighting for. You fought up to this point, so why don't you fight to stay together? so why not get the desire to fix whatever is wrong and make it last forever?

When it comes to sex, it's the bonus in the relationship not what makes the relationship. "Oh, yes, daddy, I like it when you do it like that. Give it to me, yes…yes…yes…It's yours, daddy. Mmm, you make me feel so good." There is nothing wrong with letting him know how he makes you feel when he is laying that pipe down. That inner goddess should be out and talking all kind of mess in your king's ear. When you say what you say, mean it. I love building my king up in the bedroom because he makes me feel so good. He makes the sexy come out of me. That goddess can be nasty if she wants to. You will be surprised what that goddess can have you doing with your king; you might do something that you never thought you would do. The goddess can surprise you; she is going to bring all that sexy out of you, so don't make no kind of attempts to stop her. Your king is going to help you do that because he is going to make you feel so good that you are not going to have a choice but to make him feel as good as you do, if not better.

Chemistry is what makes the relationship. Everything you went through to make the relationship work are the building blocks and the glue that hold it together. You are one with each other. You are the mirror to each other; there is not one without the other. You depend on each other for certain things; you are the Bonnie to his Clyde, the hammer to the nail, two peas in a pod, the peanut butter and jelly, yin and yang, you get the point.

You both should be comfortable enough to talk about sex openly, honestly, and comfortably with each other. You should be able to express to each other what it is that you want, i.e., things that you want to try, something that you saw in the store, something that you saw in a porn flick, something that came to mind, something that you have been dreaming about, some, the thoughts that enter your mind.

Whatever the deal is, you need to let your significant other know. No, secrets don't leave each other in the dark; being left in the dark leads to skepticism and other problems. Ladies, we talked earlier about how we sit down with our girls and talked about the best sex we had in the past, so we should be able to sit down with our men and tell them every desire that we have.

It's so important for your partner to know what it is that you want when it comes to sex. I don't care how freaky you think you are or what wild imagination you have. Nothing is going to get freaky unless you two both communicate with each other on what it is that you want when it comes down to sex. Your significant other might surprise you! Sex ain't better than love. When you and your significant other are in the middle of having sex, get intimate with each other: stare into each other's eyes, caress each other, let him or her feel all of you. Make each other want each other; tease her, tease him. There is nothing better than making love to the person you love most.

I have had a secret for quite a while that I have not told my partner about. I told him that I do have a secret and it is sexual, but it's my own fantasy secret. I want him to be able to figure out my secret without me telling him what it is. I know that sounds crazy, but it's my own fantasy. The only hint I have given him is that it pertains to sex; that is the only hint that I can give him, and believe it or not, he has almost made my fantasy come true. The only way I will tell him what that fantasy is, is by us getting married. That would be the only way that I spill the beans. I know I have said not to keep secrets because keeping secrets can and will cause problems. In my case, I told him I had a secret that I could not tell him about and what it pertained to, so therefore, we don't have any secrets with each other.

Nothing is better than making love with your mate after you both have talked about what it is that you want from each other. I don't care how silly it makes you feel to fulfill the desires of your significant other. Eventually, you are going to get comfortable. Remember, you are letting the sexy n u out and letting her do her thing. You, men, in return, are in for a night of ecstasy. This is not really about you anymore; this is about the goddess that is inside you. She is the one that needs to be running the show; she needs to be the one that shows you the way on how to please the king that you have. This is the time for her to show out and let the king see what it is that he has. That sexy n u out is all that the king wants to see and then watch how he won't be able to get enough.

Sex is the best bonus of the relationship. It's not the glue or the mortar that keeps it together; it's the fun part. You both get exercise, orgasms, and ultimate satisfaction out of it. It should be fun and entertaining for the both of you. Never let sex be a job or work, so don't make it that way. Do it all over the house: steps, washer, kitchen (with food involved), living room, dining room hallway, bathroom, shower, tub, hot tub, pool, basement, basement steps, outside in the backyard, in the car, on the car—just about anywhere and everywhere. Have fun with sex; wake up the fun inside of you and in sex itself. Remember when you were a teenager and you did it just to do it no matter what? Get that back in your life again and relive all the fun you used to have. Don't be careless with it and get caught by the authorities; be mindful but have fun.

You should even take pictures, make videos, mark it on the calendar, write a journal about it. Play some sexy music to keep the mood going. Talk to your partner about the lovely night you both had together. Ask to see what you want to improve or do better in, what more you would like to explore, and what other adventures you can have with sex.

There is nothing wrong with having a mirror in the room to watch the both of you making love. Incorporate having things in the bedroom with you, i.e., ice for when your bodies get hot or a fruit roll-up to wrap around his manhood so you can suck it off (that will keep your mouth wet and watering). Halls is always good to have as well (especially for the man while he's tasting you).

Your man/significant other is supposed to have your nose wide open. You can call it pussy whipped or dick whipped if you want to, but truth of the matter is, it's so much more than that. Remember you are a unit, so you are as ONE.

You do need time and space to be with your girls for a night, and he also needs his time and space to be with the boys for a night. You can get together at each other's house just to talk and kick back. Have a glass of wine or a stiff drink, but don't get too inebriated to where you can't walk, talk, or see straight. You both should be hanging out with people of the same caliber as yourselves, i.e., married couples or couples in long-term relationships. Don't hang out with those that are single. Single people live a different life and can steer you in the wrong direction. Some of those that you call friends that are single can also try to sabotage what you have, especially when you are happy. Now don't forget people to have angles. Although you may not think this person you trust would do anything to destroy what you have, you would be surprised at how your friends can have you fooled.

INTERMISSION
THE END

She's in the bedroom getting undressed; her husband/signifi-cant other is still at work, finishing up some paperwork for his last project. She decides to go and run some nice hot bathwater and put some lavender oil in so she can soak and relax. She ties her hair up in a bun, grabs her robe, and puts it on. She hangs up her suit in the closet and gets out another suit for tomorrow; she has a presentation to do at ten thirty in the morning, so she wants to be relaxed and well rested. It's been a tough and stressful week for her to get through, but she managed to get things done with the help of her loving husband.

She gets in the tub with a sigh of relief, covers her eyes with a warm towel, and relaxes in the essence of the lavender, which is so relaxing. She dozes off to sleep, relieving all tension in her body. The water and lavender on her skin feels so good, making her soft and silky. She wakes up from her nap, takes the towel off her eyes, and rubs her hand all over her body, feeling the silkiness of the water and oil on her skin. She sits up to let the water out and grabs her towel; she wraps the towel around her body and heads to the bedroom to sit at the vanity. She then grabs the lotion and caresses herself and puts the softening lotion on her skin. She starts with her legs and works her way up to her neck. As she put the lotion on, she thinks about her husband and how he makes her feel at the touch of his hand. She takes the towel off her head and lays it across the bench; she then turns off the lights and climbs into the bed. She continues to think about her husband, and it gets her in the mood to feel him inside of her, so she decides to amuse herself and starts the journey to semi-ecstasy. Her body temperature rises with the thoughts of her husband, and his manhood fill her mind—the way he feels inside of her and how he kisses her on her breast, the way his tongue feels on her clitoris and the sucking of her juices, and he makes her secrete her sweet juices. She becomes satisfied with what she has done with herself and falls asleep.

He walks in quietly in the hallway, making sure not to wake up anyone in the house. He reaches her door and slowly pushes it open, keeping himself unseen with all the dark clothes he has on. He notices the way she is breathing, consistent, which tells him that she is sound asleep. He walks in quietly, placing his black bag on the floor and slowly starts to take off his clothes. He unfastens his belt and takes it off first, placing it on the floor, careful not to let it drop. He then takes off his shirt, letting it fall to the floor, along with his pants. He leaves himself with his T-shirt and socks on. He walks over to her to look at her naked body lying on the bed. He can smell the quintessence of her skin, and she smells exceptional. He gazes at her body, being careful not to touch her; he does not want to wake her. He then walks quietly back to his black bag he placed on the floor, unzips the bag, and pulls out all the necessities in which he is going to need to secure her. He has in his possession a ball gag, rope, blindfold, and spreader. He's been watching her for a long time, and she is the one that he wants. Her eyes are small and sexy, her face is of an Egyptian nature, and her body is of unexplainable beauty. He places on rope on each of the four poles of the bed, measuring them long enough to reach her hands and ankles. He places her first ankle ever so gently inside the rope, being careful not to disturb her. He then goes to the other side to do the same. She moves but doesn't wake. He thinks to himself that this is the most bizarre thing he has ever done, but he's never wanted someone so much and he's never desired someone so much that he went to this extreme.

He has on a mask, so she can't see his face; he walks over to the bed with blindfold and ball gag in hand. He first grabs her and covers her mouth so she won't scream. She wakens and struggles, but he proceeds to climb on top of her, overpowering her, and first blindfolds her, holding both her hands above her head. He then proceeds to get her wrists in the ropes that he has placed on the poles of the bed, securing her so she can't fight back. She starts to scream, which leads him to place the gag over her mouth. He turns on the light on the nightstand and looks at her, in her dismay, struggling to get free and stares at the nakedness of her body, feeling her smooth and ever so decadent skin. She continues to struggle, trying to get out of her restraints to no avail. He doesn't say a word to her; he just sits on top of her and watches.

He gets up and pulls the covers back to the end of the bed to see all her body. He climbs on the bed, starting from the bottom, and rubs his hand over her legs, slowly going up to her thighs. He starts to kiss her inner thigh, spreading her legs to see her ladihood. He then starts to kiss it slowly, then he begins to suck on it, feeling her breast. She tries to fight it, but it feels so good; the sensation of his lips and tongue on her makes her secrete. He keeps going, making her feel so good, and she can't help but give in to him. The way he is making her feel is desired. Her not being able to see is making it suspenseful, but knowing she can't do anything about it makes her fight the feeling, but it's to no avail.

He sucks and bites her on her leg and then goes back in to make her feel the pleasure she needs to feel, still squeezing on her breast. He blows on her kitty cat so she can feel a little breeze. He then goes in for a little more, making her squirm and moan in such pleasure that it turns him on. He stops giving her oral pleasure and kisses and sucks his way up to her stomach while placing two fingers inside of her to keep her coming and to keep her wet. He suck on her stomach, coming up to her breasts. He places her nipple inside his mouth and sucks on it, one breast at a time and biting her nipple ever so gently. He then makes his way back down between her legs and pulls out his fingers and places his hard penis inside of her nice and slow so she can feel all of him. She wants to gasp, but she can't. All she can do is make noises with the gag being in her mouth.

He strokes her slowly, going deeper and deeper with each stroke. She's so overwhelmed with his manhood that her body temperature rises and she gets hot. It feels so good to her she tries to stroke him back, but all she can do is come up to him a little bit, and he watches her in amazement and decides to pull himself out. He caresses her body and decides that he is going to take his time with her and play with her for a while. He ravishes her, like a mountain lion who caught his prey. He sucks on her neck, grips her breast with some authority, makes his way to her ear, and bites and pulls on her lobe. It feels so good to her, and she wants so desperately to say something, but she can't. Her body wants him; she likes feeling his hands all over her body. The way he smells is intensifying. It feels so good to her that she doesn't know what to do; she's tied to the bed, gagged and can't move the way she wants to move. All she can do is moan while her body shakes with ecstasy and pleasure. She had no idea that she could feel this good; she had no idea that this man could make her feel like she is on top of the world and nothing else matters. There are no other thoughts in her head but the desire to have more of this immeasurable pleasure she's feeling.

He gets up and goes to the foot of the bed where he left his bag and grabs the spreader bar. He makes his way back over to her and unties one of her ankles and places it inside of the spreader bar and proceeds to do the other ankle. He goes to untie one of her wrists and guides her to side of the bed; he gives her the notion that he wants her to bend down, and she does just that. He places her wrist inside the spreader bar and locks her in. He then unties her other wrist and proceeds to do the same. He picks her up and carries her to the middle of the room and puts her down. He stares at her body shimmering in the light, glistening like a piece of licked candy. He admires every inch of her body, touching and kissing her on her ass. He proceeds to kiss and then licks it, causing her to moan with passion.

It feels so good to her it sends waves and shocks through her body; she doesn't know how to handle it, so she screams with passion the best way she can. Oh, the passion she feels that she's never felt before. Not being able to see, talk, or move is making her want him even more. It turns her on in a way she's never felt before and it feels good. He continues to eat her out from behind, tasting all of her. She is nice and wet and ready for him to enter her. He grabs a handful of hair and enters her, giving her all of him, stroking her deep, and slow slapping her on her ass. He grunts; she feels so good to him, pulling him back in as he strokes. He smacks her on the ass again, going deeper. She moans, and as she moans, she gets wetter. He places one finger inside her ass and penetrates it with his finger, giving her a sensation she's never felt before. It was strange to her at first, but with him stroking her at the same time, it feels good to her, making her want more. She is in pure ecstasy and doesn't know how to express that. He continues to penetrate her, noticing that the more he penetrates, the wetter she is getting.

He pulls himself out because he's not ready to release; he walks over to the side of her and lies on the floor and starts to suck on her breast, fingering her at the same time so she can continue to receive pleasure. He sucks on her breast, giving her a little pain at the same time. He then gets up and lays her on the floor, and she's spread like an eagle, waiting for him to enter. He not only enters her, but he also enters the very part he violated with his finger. He takes it slow, with the juices flowing from the front going down to her backside. He slowly makes his way all the way in and strokes her gently but slowly until she starts to secrete from behind. His tempo moves up, and she's not in pain. She wants to play with herself from the sensations she's getting, but she is bound and can't move. He keeps stroking her and smacking her ass, going faster and deeper and sending her to a realm she's never been to before.

He pulls out and places himself inside of her wetness, which is so much wetter than before. He strokes her hard and deep, making her scream with pleasure and passion, her body sweaty and hot. She has discovered an unfathomable amount of passion in this moment; she's never felt this way, and she loves it, not wanting the night to end. He decides he wants to let her hands free, so he unbinds her hands to let her stand up. He then also unbinds her ankles to let her free, knowing that she is not going to run. He takes her and throws her up against the wall with her face facing him. He ravishes her like he has never done before. Her legs wrap around his waist, and she pulls him in closer to her, feeling on his smooth skin. His body feels of a god. He's wet from sweating and feels so muscular, hard, and defined. That turns her on more so. He thrashes her, with her still being blindfolded. Not wanting to take the blindfold off, she accepts all of him and how he is making her feel. He's so deep inside of her she can't even make a noise. Her mouth is parched; she wants to kiss on him and suck his lovely feeling body, and knowing that she can't do any of these things makes her want him more. He puts her down and picks her up so she is hanging upside down, and he starts to give her oral pleasure, and she feels the hardness of his penis and places it in her mouth to return the favor. He's making her legs shake like they are having spasms. She sucks on him, making his legs weak, but he doesn't give in. He keeps going, knowing that she's giving it to him the same way he's giving it to her. Her body wants to explode from what she is feeling from him. Her legs are shaking uncontrollably, and she can feel herself getting ready to squirt.

He teases her with his tongue, and she finally gives way and squirts, shooting a stream of nectar in the air, which comes down her backside. It gets in her hair, on her neck, back, on him. She can't believe she let go in such a way. It was erotic and also a first for her. He then places her on the bed and places her knees next to her ears and goes in balls deep, making sure that she can feel every inch of his hardness. It feels so good to him that all her nectar are all over his penis, legs, and stomach. He's starting to power drive her, giving her no room to take a breath or catch a break. He wants her to have that orgasm. He wants to have an orgasm, and he wants them both to come at the same time. She's wet, creamy, sticky, and getting weaker by the minute. She knows she is about to climax, but she's not ready because it feels so good to her.

He turns her over and puts her up on her knees on the bed, and he inserts himself back into her. He decides to take her gag off, leaving the blindfold on. He pulls a handful of hair, strokes her, and smacks her on the ass. She begins to stroke him back. It becomes a tempo; they are both feeling good. It's good to her, and she feels good to him. He grabs her ass and pulls her to him, spreads her cheeks apart to look at her, and decides to finger her anally. She's not sure what to do with all the feelings that are going through her body. All she can do is moan, get hot, and give it back to him harder. He grabs her hands, motioning for her to grab his legs while he thrusts her. She grabs the pillow and bites the pillow, feeling all his manhood. He begins to play with her clit, and it sends her into overdrive. She's not sure what to do. She feels uncontrollable. The way he is making her feel she's never felt before, but it feels so good.

They proceed to continue thrusting each other, and he can feel himself about to come, so he turns her over on her back and pulls her to the edge of the bed. She, in turn, helps him get her adjusted, and he places one leg on his shoulder and the other one he takes with his hand to spread her leg apart from the other. He can feel all of her, and he is hitting her G-spot. She's about to orgasm. She screams out, "Right there, don't stop, don't move, ohh, ohh, ohh." And she releases, he releases. They are both in ecstasy, coming at the same time. He lets out a gasp of relief. He's sweaty and wet, and she's sweaty, wet, and sticky. There's a wet spot going down the side of the bed. He lies on the side of her. She takes off the blindfold and tells her husband, "Baby, that was so good. I enjoyed every moment of that delightful ravenous experience." He says to her, "I did too. It was, by far, the craziest thing we have ever done." They fall asleep in each other's arms, not able to move.

CONGRATULATIONS! You have now reached the end of the book! I would like to take the time out to thank you for supporting me the purchase of this book. I hope you got something out of this book which was helpful to you and your spouse. I have included a few things at the end for the purpose of having fun and to give you a few ideas which may help you along the way. You will also see the questionnaire I used to get feedback. I hope you will have a better understanding of what's to come, what you can expect of one another and become a better prosperous couple than you were before. It was my own little study I did for this book, so hopefully you will have a better understanding of what's to come, what has passed, and what you have to look forward to. Thank you so much for reading, and I hope you got more than you bargained for!

Here is a list of music I compiled together just to give you an idea of how you can set the mood. Some people may have heard of them and some might have not. This is like a guideline of what you can use, depending on your style, rhythm, etc. Of course, you can always make a list for yourself. Put a playlist together on your iPad, iPod, android, or whatever you have so when you are ready, so is your music. I have also included a few hints on the side of some of the music just to give you an idea of what the song can be used for. You can always change it up as you see fit or adjust your own playlist.

Music

"Better Half of Me"—Monifah
"Body Party"—Ciara (nice private dance song)
"Dance for You"—Beyonce (nice private song)
"Explode"—TGT
"Feel Like Makin' Love"—D'Angelo
"Gorilla"—Bruno Mars (nice starter song during or after dinner)
"Kiss and Make up"—Chris Bender
"Last Chance"—Genuwine
"Make It Last Forever"—Keith Sweat
"Make Love"—Keri Hilson
"Make That Sound"—J. Holiday
"Motivation"—Kelly Rowland (nice private dance song)
"Nice and Slow"—Usher
"Overdose"—Jamie Foxx
"Pouring Like Rain"—Chris Bender
"Raindrops"—Jeremih (mood setter)
"Representin'"—Ludacris (rap)
"Say It"—Ne Yo (mood setter)
"Scream"—Tank *(when you call yourself mad, listen to this song)* put
    on repeat if need be
"Sex Me"—R. Kelly
"Sex Never Felt Better"—TGT
"Sex You Up"—Color Me Badd (nice starter song during or after
    dinner)
"Slave"—Tony Thompson (nice starter song during or after dinner)
"Slow Dance"—Keri Hilson

"Storm (Forecass)"—Jamie Foxx
"Suga, Suga"—Monifah
"Sweet Love"—Chris Brown
"The Way"—Jill Scott
"T-Shirt and Panties"—Adina Howard
"Uhh Ahh"—Boyz II Men
"Waiter/The 5 Senses"—Jeremih
"Wanna Be Close"—Avant
"Wanna Make Love"—Blackstreet
"Wet the Bed"—Chris Brown (nice starter song during or after dinner)

I also have a few websites compiled for you to take a look at in case you need some help or want to get right to it:

*Cirillas.com
*Ambiance
*Adameeve.com
**Yandy.com
*Fredericks.com
*Lingerediva.com
*Edenfantasys.com
*Forplaycatalog.com
*Spurst.com
*Spiceylingerie.com
*Herroom.com

Ones that I have ordered from before
*** Ones that I really liked for lingerie**

You may even try to go to the nearest adult store in your area. If they don't have some of the items that you are looking for, you can always find them somewhere on the net (including from one of the sites I have listed above).

References

Merriam-Webster's Dictionary

http://www.psychologytoday.com/blog/is-psychology-making-us-sick/201310/building-repairing-trust-keys-sustainable-relationship

http://www.wikihow.com/Build-Trust-in-a-Relationship

http://www.webmd.com/sex-relationships/guide/sex-and-health?page=3

http://www.medicinenet.com/sexual_health_pictures_slideshow/article.htm

http://www.utexas.edu/news/2007/07/31/psychology/

Survey

1. How many times this year have you cheated on your significant other?
2. How many times have you lied about cheating?
3. How many times have you lied so you won't hurt your significant other's feelings?
4. Why did you cheat?
5. What drives you to cheat?
6. What do you feel you are lacking in sex?
7. Do you feel you satisfy your partner?
8. Does your partner satisfy you?
9. Are you satisfied with your sexual experience?
10. What would you change about the sex you're having?
11. Do you feel or think you will cheat?
12. Do you have any secrets you are keeping from your significant other?
13. Is there anything about the sex you're having you would like to improve?
14. When having sex, do you like to talk dirty?
15. Do you like it when you are talked dirty to?
16. Do you like to be dominated in the bedroom?
17. Do you like to role-play?
18. Do you feel like you are being cheated on?
19. Do you think of other people while you are having sex with your significant other?
20. Have you been pleased the way you want to be pleased?
21. Are you happy in your relationship?

22. If your partner did not do oral sex and would only have sex in two to three positions, would that keep you satisfied?
23. Do you talk to your partner about your sex life?
24. If you could lie to save your relationship, would you?

I would just like to take a time out to say thank you to you for taking some time out for yourself. Writing this book was an experience for me. I am glad I was able to do what I wanted to do in life which was write. I hope it had meaning to you. I hope it didn't come across in a negative way at all. One thing you have to do in life is keep pushing on and keep your head up no matter how bad the storm is. Truth is, you learn from the storms you go through in life. You just have to pay attention to what you are supposed to get out of it. Most things in life are easier said than done, but if you get enough courage to keep going no matter what gives you the courage, then do so. Not all our marriages or relationships always work out the way we want them to, but as long as you both put 100 percent of yourself in what you are doing to help the relationship, then you are, in turn, going to get something back—Satisfaction.

By all means, enjoy life and what it has to offer. Enjoy each other because no one is promised tomorrow. Remember to take time out for yourself and each other.

Peace, love, and happiness,
L. Childs

About the Author

The author, L. Childs, was born in Grand Rapids, Michigan, and later moved to Akron, Ohio. She went to Garfiled High School where she did not graduate but later got her GED. Sometime later, she gave birth to her first child at a young age where life was beginning to unfold. She then later gave birth to four more children while experiencing what life had to offer. She got a job in corporate America and started juggling work, parenting, passion for alcohol, obsession for sex, and the desire to find the balance in it all.

As life has shown her how it can be, she's made the best out of all her situations she's been presented with. Bad choices made their way into her life, and she took them and did the best she could with them. She discovered later on, through the pain and heartache, that she had become a sex addict. She then decided to write a book on what life has shown and taught her. Hoping someone would be able to relate to the things she has been through in life, she finally decided to air out her laundry, get some closure, and come to peace with all that has gone on and taken place in and throughout her journey.

Later down the road, she became a grandmother to three beautiful granddaughters. She became a truck driver and is currently working on another novel with special thanks to life.